Gaby

There she was, after nine long years.

Funny, that—when he should remember only her desertion—apparently the boy who had loved her so foolishly and fully still lived inside Eli Wolverton.

Craved to see her face again.

Just one time, before…

Dear Reader,

I'm drawn to the strong, haunted hero, the man who will face danger and who will sacrifice what he yearns for most, in order to do what is right for those he loves. A man like Eli Wolverton.

Eli has already made that sacrifice once before. Framed by the man who murdered Eli's mother, he walked away from Gaby Navarro without a word. Broke her heart, in order to protect her. Now he's back, accused of another crime, the object of an intense manhunt. The safest choice is to leave, but he won't.

Because this time, the only way to protect Gaby is to stay near her. Even though she has no reason to believe in him. Soul mates parted, then reunited... with long odds against them...yum. Love this stuff!

I hope you'll enjoy this sequel to my novel *Mercy*, where you first met Gaby as Mona Gerard Fitzgerald's assistant. And for those of you who've written me about my DEEP IN THE HEART series, well... read on. There's a little surprise for you in Gaby and Eli's story.

I love hearing from readers, either by post at P. O. Box 3000 #79, Georgetown, TX 78628 or via my Web site, www.jeanbrashear.com, or at www.eHarlequin.com.

Thank you so much for all your lovely letters and e-mails. It is an enormous privilege to be allowed to share with you, through my stories, my deep conviction that love is the most powerful force in the world. I wish love and all blessings to every one of you.

All my best,

Jean

RETURN TO WEST TEXAS

Jean Brashear

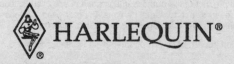

TORONTO • NEW YORK • LONDON
AMSTERDAM • PARIS • SYDNEY • HAMBURG
STOCKHOLM • ATHENS • TOKYO • MILAN • MADRID
PRAGUE • WARSAW • BUDAPEST • AUCKLAND

ISBN-13: 978-0-373-78158-4
ISBN-10:   0-373-78158-X

RETURN TO WEST TEXAS

ABOUT THE AUTHOR

A letter to Rod Stewart resulting in a Cinderella birthday for her daughter sowed the seeds of Jean Brashear's writing career. Since becoming published two years after she started her first book, she has appeared on the Waldenbooks bestseller list and been a finalist for or won numerous awards, including the RITA® Award, the *Romantic Times BOOKreviews* Reveiwers' Choice, National Readers Choice and others. A lifelong avid reader, she still finds it thrilling each time she sees her name on the cover of a new book.

Books by Jean Brashear

HARLEQUIN SUPERROMANCE
1071–WHAT THE HEART WANTS
1105–THE HEALER
1142–THE GOOD DAUGHTER
1190–A REAL HERO
1219–MOST WANTED
1251–COMING HOME
1267–FORGIVENESS
1339–SWEET MERCY

SIGNATURE SELECT SAGA
MERCY

To my own military hero, Ercel G. Brashear,
U.S. Marine Corps, Vietnam, and to the men of
our two families who have served our country: my
late father, Edward R. Roberson, U.S. Navy; my
brother, Edward R. Roberson Jr., U.S. Air Force; my
father-in-law, George Ercel Brashear, U.S. Army; my
brothers-in-law, Dennis West, U.S. Air Force, and
Steven Brashear, U.S. Army Special Forces.

And to the men and women of our military forces,
past and present, for the many sacrifices they and
their families have made to protect us all.

I am humbled by your courage.

ACKNOWLEDGMENTS

My heartfelt thanks to Captain Ryan Kendall,
U.S. Army, for generously sharing his time and
expertise to help me make Eli a wizard in fieldcraft
without the benefit of military service. Thanks,
Ryan, for leaping into the spirit of brainstorming so
readily and skillfully—and for answering my constant
stream of questions! (P.S. A big hi to Shannon.)

Many thanks, as well, to Steve and Susie Sadler, for
answering all manner of horse questions and for
sharing the pleasure of Spika and her pasture mates
with my mother on one fine day at the farm.

Any errors made or liberties taken
are strictly my own.

CHAPTER ONE

"YOU DID IT, GIRLFRIEND! I'm so proud of you."

Gaby Navarro accepted a hug from her ebullient friend, Beth Thom. "I keep wanting to pinch myself." Though, truth was, she'd burned a lot of midnight oil to get this promotion to style editor at *Bijou* magazine.

"It's real hot stuff," Beth advised. "The boss better watch out or you'll have her job."

"I think she's safe for a day or two." Gaby wondered why, now that she had what she'd battled so hard to obtain, she didn't feel more jubilant. From the day she'd left college and arrived in Manhattan, she'd been focused on exactly this climb. She was only tired; that was all.

"We have to celebrate tonight. I'm making reservations." Beth's cheer was impossible to resist. "Put yourself in my hands, girl. We will have a rip-roaring time."

Gaby found herself smiling. Letting the sense of accomplishment sink in. "Thank you."

"Hey, I'm selfish. Editorial board meetings are a pain in the you-know-what. I could use a partner in crime."

Gaby laughed.

The phone on her desk buzzed. She glanced at it, then at Beth. Sighed. "Back to the real world."

Beth grinned. "No rest for the wicked." With a wink, she departed.

Gaby picked up the receiver. "Yes?"

"There's a call for you from Texas," the receptionist said. "A Sheriff Anderson. He refuses to leave a message. Congratulations, by the way."

Sheriff Anderson? It had been nine years since she'd had contact with anyone back there.

"Okay, I'll take the call. And thanks."

She punched the flickering button. "Gaby Navarro."

"Gabriela?" So strange to be called Gabriela once more. And the voice was not the older one she'd expected. This was his son, Chad. Her former boyfriend.

"Chad? You're…the sheriff?"

He chuckled. "Amazing, huh? My dad passed away two years ago, and the voters saw fit to give me the job." Memories crashed in on her…. Chad, the golden boy, literally. Blond, tall and handsome. Quarterback of the football team, student-body president. All that a girl could dream of.

Until Eli had changed everything.

"Gabriela, I'm sorry, but this isn't a social call. I'm afraid I have bad news."

The past vanished with the warning in his tone. "Papa is all right, isn't he?"

A long silence. "That's why I'm calling. You need to come home."

"Is he sick? Hurt?" Papa had always seemed invincible.

"I wish I didn't have to do this on the phone. No easy way to break it. Your father is gone, Gabriela."

"Gone?" she echoed. She dropped into her chair and opened the middle desk drawer, then groped for the picture she kept there.

"There was a fire in one of the barns. He was alone."

"Where was Ramón?" The foreman had been with her father as long as she could remember.

A pause. "Your father had to let Ramón go several months back, so there was no one—" He cleared his throat. "By the time a passerby noticed the smoke, it was too late."

She hunched over her desk, clutching the photograph. She'd left Texas in a fury. Thrown ugly words in her father's face, and now they would never—

She barely registered what Chad was saying. "…Good man, but in the last few years, his health had deteriorated."

The knife slid in a little deeper. "I'll be on the first plane."

"Let me know which flight, and I'll pick you up."

"No, I—"

"Gabriela, please. I want to help you."

"I have to go now. I'll take care of it." She hung up before he could tell her anything else.

Before she had to hear more recrimination in his voice. Her father had wanted her to marry Chad and unite their adjoining ranches.

But she'd had other dreams, even before—

Eli. Outcast Eli Wolverton had been her dark secret.

Her one true love.

Or so she'd believed until he'd abandoned her. Vanished under a cloud of suspicion.

Eli was old history now, not worth a second's thought, but Papa…

What have I done?

She stroked one finger across the photo of Papa and herself on her seventh birthday, a dignified man smiling at the girl in the pink organdy dress. Ruthlessly, she pushed back the black demon that would devour her if she thought about never being able to make up for what she'd done to her father.

Stop it. Focus on the details. Get online and find a plane ticket. With a leaden heart, she reached for her keyboard drawer.

"Hey, girl, I got us— What's wrong?" Beth at the door.

Gaby couldn't figure out how to answer her. She'd never told a soul how she and her father had parted. She'd left her past behind in Texas.

"I just—" She crumpled. "My—my

father—he's—" She lifted stinging eyes. "He's dead."

"Oh, honey…" In minutes, Beth had the whole story and, in her inimitable mode, had swung into action. Before Gaby could blink, she was booked on a flight leaving in three hours and tucked into a cab, headed to pack her things and return home.

Except it hadn't been home for nine years.

And now it never would be.

ELI WOLVERTON MADE certain he'd left no tracks leading to the cave where he'd taken up residence. He knelt before the scarred and emaciated dog that seemed to have adopted him and untied the rope he'd used to restrain the healing animal while out making his rounds in the darkness.

With a practiced eye, he scanned the wounds the dog had suffered at the hands of the worst of predators: Eli's fellow man. As he'd traveled the globe the past nine years, Eli had learned that human nature was the same the world over: rich or impoverished, educated or illiterate, there was cruelty in mankind, though there was astonishing courage and kindness, as well.

He'd also acquired critical survival skills to add to those he'd learned the hard way as a child dodging his mother's boyfriend's fists. He could forage for food from jungle to desert, collect water from the dew or the underside of leaves, even perform basic medical care, if necessary. Though he'd experienced enough violence to last him a lifetime, he knew how to take a punch and throw one. He was a fair shot and could use a knife. He preferred, however, to wield his laptop and camera as he circled the planet, telling the stories of people without voices. Making their plights heard on his Internet report, *The Hot Spot Journal.*

The wandering life suited him fine. He was happiest alone. Relying on no one.

The only person he'd truly trusted, besides the mother he hadn't been able to help when it had counted, was Gaby Navarro.

And she'd abandoned him when he'd needed her most.

The dog licked his hand.

Eli stroked him as he eyed the empty dish. "Your appetite's improving. You ready for a trip outside?"

As if he understood, the dog rose and stretched. Wagged the stub of tail.

Eli smiled. "It's hotter than Hades out there already. Don't guess you want to wait for evening?"

The animal, an odd mix of a boxer's muscular frame, however malnourished, and beagle ears and coloring, whimpered.

Eli headed toward the slit that was the well-disguised mouth of the cave. "All right, let's go."

The dog he had yet to name because he had no intention of keeping him made surprisingly good time, beating him outside. Eli could almost hear the sigh of relief as the hound lifted his leg on a creosote bush. "You're nearly ready, fella. If only I had a clue what to do with you."

A pet was not in his plans. Nor was any sort of permanence.

As the dog followed his nose, Eli settled into the cool, welcome shade and stared out at the blistering heat shimmering over a landscape some would term barren.

He had once called it home, a place he'd missed more than he would ever have imagined at eighteen. It had its own beauty, sere and harsh as it was. The scent of creosote bush and mesquite, the endless vista, the foothills topped by a sky big and blue, with only the faintest vein of cloud-white to marble it.

This land demanded much of those who would inhabit it. The faint of heart moved on—east to the Hill Country, north to the cool green mountains of southern New Mexico—or traversed the thousand miles of more desert to reach the Pacific Ocean.

As he had, nine years ago. Hitchhiked and camped out, worked a series of menial jobs with an eye to making it to California. Gotten a ride from a television reporter, Bob Collier, who'd been driving cross-country, collecting the stories of ordinary people. Their pace had been slow, and as they'd traveled, he and Bob had talked about all the places Bob had been, what he'd seen through thirty years of globetrotting, how the business of news had changed. Bob had opened up the world to Eli, though neither he nor Bob had realized it at the time.

Since then, he'd ranged far and wide to escape the death sentence waiting for him here, however unofficially.

Because he'd known too much. Seen too much.

And been powerless to save Gaby except by leaving her behind.

He'd written her a note after everything had gone wrong that last night. He'd longed to see her just once more before he vanished. Be sure she didn't doubt that he was innocent.

But Gaby had never shown. She'd obviously figured out what he'd understood from the first, even if he'd ignored it for one heady span—that they had no future. She'd had plans, big ones, and he was all too aware that, whatever she'd said back then, he did not fit in them.

At first, the pain of losing her had nearly killed him. If you could die from missing the other half of yourself, he'd have been a goner.

Anger had saved him. Brick by brick, he'd rebuilt the walls only Gaby had breached.

Life went on, and so had he.

And he almost managed to forget Gaby—though she wasn't called Gaby now, he was sure. That had been his name for her, while everyone else used Gabriela, a graceful, dignified choice for a girl everyone expected to go far.

His jaw cracked in a yawn as the long, strenuous night caught up with him. He whistled for the dog, which came running. Eli poured more water in the animal's makeshift dish and briefly contemplated eating something himself.

But in the end, he simply drank water, too, checked his sleeping bag for unwelcome visitors and stretched out.

The dog padded toward the mouth of the cave as if to keep watch. Still musing over what might have become of the young girl who'd been the only one to find something worthwhile in a hellion, Eli let himself slip away into slumber.

GABY WALKED THROUGH the Jetway and felt the press of dry West Texas heat. She proceeded to baggage claim, hearing around her soft-spoken Spanish and West Texas twang. The faces, so many a dusky gold like her own, brought a lump to her throat.

Chilis. Here, even in the airport, she smelled their tang, underlain by the sweet, floury scent of tortillas on the griddle, the rich aroma of frijoles and garlic and onion. Her mouth watered, and she had an urge to stop at the little kiosk and stuff herself with the flavors of home.

After nine years on the East Coast, she'd forgotten so much. She moved through the crowds with a smile creasing her face.

Until the thought, never far away, reappeared.

Oh, Papa.

"Gabriela?" The baritone voice, richer than she'd registered in those shocked minutes on the phone.

"Chad." Jeans and boots and starched khaki shirt, a Stetson, quickly removed from his head as all true cowboys were raised to do. His bright gold hair had darkened to honey. "How did you know when I'd arrive?"

"I have my sources." He smiled.

"I can't ask you to—"

"You don't have to. I'm here, Gabriela. Just lean on me for a bit."

His shoulders certainly appeared wide enough.

But she wasn't into leaning. She grabbed her bag before he could and followed him outside to the big, shiny black extended-cab pickup.

"You always owned a sports car." Why had she remembered that now? He'd arrived for dates with her in a never-ending series of slick racers.

And had tried to seduce her in every one.

Chad laughed. "I still like them. Got one in the garage, in fact—a Corvette. But this is more practical for my job."

She flicked a glance toward his shirt pocket. "No badge?"

"Not to pick up a pretty lady." He grinned as he helped her into the seat.

"I'm amazed, Chad. I never realized you wanted to follow in your dad's footsteps."

A faint shadow darkened his blue eyes briefly. "I didn't, but—" He shrugged. "Things change." He shut her door and rounded the hood.

They rode in silence for a few minutes. "Hungry? We could stop at Seis Salsas."

Wistfully, she considered the legendary restaurant. Wondered if sharing a meal with an attractive man was disrespectful to her father's memory.

Given that it was this particular man, she guessed her father would be smiling.

But despite the moment of temptation

back at the terminal, she wasn't really hungry, even having had no lunch. Wasn't sure she ever would be.

"Thanks, but I'd rather get this over with."

"No sweat." He hooked one wrist over the steering wheel and hit the accelerator, driving fast and confidently as he always had. "Why don't you just settle back and catch a nap." Chamizal was nearly two hours away.

"I look that bad?"

He glanced over at her. "Men in New York too blind to tell you you're beautiful?"

She found a smile at that. "It's not that simple to meet a straight man who's not married, whether to a woman or to his work. Or both." She lifted a shoulder. "But that's okay. I'm focused on my career."

"So no one for me to tussle with over you?"

Tussle. The word provoked a chuckle. "Nope." When was the last time she'd said *nope?* "But I won't be here long enough, anyway."

"I might like to change your mind on that topic."

"You can't. There's nothing for me here.

I just have to figure out how to dispose of—" Everything her father had spent a lifetime building. Anguish flooded her. That land had been in her family for decades. After all her mother's miscarriages, her father's dream had been for her to carry on the legacy.

Oh, Papa, I can't.

Chad squeezed her shoulder. "We'll talk about all that later. You can count on me—I hope you know that. But for now, just close your eyes and let me get you home."

Home. That word again.

Exhausted, Gaby merely nodded and complied.

Only seconds had passed, she would swear, before the truck stopped.

"Gabriela." Chad touched her arm.

Dread rose as she resisted opening her eyes.

"We're at your house, honey. You don't have to sleep here, though. You could stay with me."

The warm invitation in his eyes was tempting, but she didn't allow herself cowardice.

She forced her eyelids apart. Felt the tears gather.

Ruthlessly, she blinked them back and examined the place where she'd spent her childhood. The stucco, once a pristine white her father had repainted every couple of years to keep it as her mother had loved it, was chipped and the color of sand. Even her inexperienced eye could detect a dip in the roof and missing shingles. Everywhere, she spotted signs of decay Frank Navarro would never have allowed.

His health was failing. "What was wrong with him?"

Chad grimaced. "Lung cancer."

Gaby's breath caught as she recalled the pipe that her father had cherished. "Was he getting medical attention?"

Chad shook his head. "I don't think so."

A desperation to run jittered inside her. She grabbed the door handle.

"Gabriela—"

She didn't wait for him. Couldn't bear to hear any more just now. As her feet settled onto once-familiar soil, she whipped her head around, searching for something, anything, to erase her guilt at the shambles she confronted.

Her gaze caught on the garden. "It needs watering." Her feet began to move before her thoughts could catch up. She had to have something constructive to do before she gave in and screamed out her grief and shame.

"Gabriela, there's something I have to tell you."

She kept walking.

"Gabriela, wait. Don't—"

She rounded the corner of the house. Saw the blackened ruin in the distance.

And fell to her knees with a moan.

Chad reached her side and lifted her.

She recoiled from the comfort. Forced herself to face the spot where her father had died. For long seconds, she couldn't muster a word as she stared at it. Then at last she did. "How?" she croaked.

Chad was silent, too, then cleared his throat. "That's what I was going to tell you." He stepped nearer. "There's no easy way to say this. The fire was set. I got confirmation just before I picked you up."

She whirled. "Arson? But—but who would—"

His expression was grim. "I wish I didn't have to cause you more pain, but you'll hear soon enough."

"Hear what?"

"Remember when Eli set the fire that killed his mother? Then escaped capture and vanished?"

"No." She covered her mouth. Shook her head violently. "You can't mean—" She began to tremble.

"Eli was spotted right here, arguing with your father only days ago. He hated your dad for coming between you. But don't you worry. If he's still in the area, I'll find him.

"And when I do—" Chad gripped her arms "—he'll be charged with your father's murder."

CHAPTER TWO

THE BANG OF THE SCREEN DOOR echoed against her already shattered nerves. At last, she'd convinced Chad to go, and she was alone.

With nothing but silence, she was left to ponder the ambitions for which she'd turned her back on her father, on his grueling work, his hopes for her. He'd never forgiven her… and now he never would.

Swallowing at the lump of congealed sobs in her throat, Gaby looked around the simple, small country kitchen. The same old fifties-era tubular metal table and chairs on which she'd eaten hundreds of meals sat behind the door. She walked to the cabinet beside the sink and took down a jelly glass she'd used a thousand times. She ran the faucet, smelling the cool, clear well water, suddenly eager to drink in its innocent purity.

As she trailed her hands across the multi-colored flecks of the Formica countertop, her gaze fastened on the brown circle left by a hot cast-iron skillet when she'd once caught the grease on fire, trying to cook a surprise birthday meal for Papa.

She set the glass down, her drink untasted.

Gaby escaped from the sharp ache of this room and its memories and entered the darkened living room, where the first thing she saw was her father's chair.

Empty.

So many moments of him sitting there rushed up to meet her—after a long day, his head leaning back in exhaustion; his holding her on his lap, letting her pretend to read the paper to him; his carefully adding cramped figures on the back of a brown paper sack in the dim lamplight, his forehead wrinkled with worry.

She made it to the chair before she fell to the floor and sobbed. Kneeling, arms still tight around her middle, she laid her cheek against the worn cushion and drew in the sweetish tang of the pipe tobacco he had loved.

She caught the rich leather scent from his saddle and rode again before him like a princess, his arm gesturing wide across their kingdom. She breathed in the loamy garden and remembered following him down the rows, biting her cheek in concentration to be sure she dropped the tiny seeds precisely into the holes his big fingers had made.

"Oh, Papa, how you must have hated me." Her stomach hurt from the twisting, sour regret. She couldn't breathe around the black knot of her guilt.

What had happened since she'd left?

Her ears rang with the echo of the last summer she ever spent in this house.

Her father's rage that night when he'd caught her sneaking out to meet Eli. Their bitter exchange when she'd told him about the scholarship that would be her ticket out of Chamizal.

Then his silence. His refusal to acknowledge her dreams, to understand that she needed to be more than a mother at eighteen, old by thirty. That she'd never wanted to fight the wind, the heat, the poverty, attempting to pull a meager living from the soil of this harsh land.

"How can you do this to me? Do you not see that I did all this for you?"

"No, Papa, you did it for *you*. You expected me to be your good little girl and go find a husband, have babies, give you grandsons. You never asked me what I wanted."

"*¡Bastante!* Enough—" he had roared, his face dark with rage.

"You're right, Papa. It is enough. I'm sick of this desolate place. I'm going away, where I can be somebody."

She'd barely heard his reply. "You are already somebody here, Gabriela Lucía. You are my daughter." He'd locked her in her room and departed.

When he'd returned, he'd sat up all night to be sure she didn't leave to meet Eli.

For hours, she'd watched at her window and waited, but Eli had never come. When day had broken and Papa had set her free, she'd searched for Eli everywhere, all the deserted places he'd made his refuge because he'd had nowhere else to go. She'd visited each spot where they'd ever hidden notes for each other, and she'd been frantic that he was waiting and wondering where she was.

Then she'd heard about Eli's mother and the fire that had claimed her life. About the manhunt going on for Eli as the prime suspect.

He'd vanished without a word to her.

Soon, it had been time for her to go, too. She nearly hadn't, but she'd kept remembering how Eli had encouraged her as she'd searched for scholarships and studied late into the night. He'd told her she could be so much more. That he was proud of her.

So Gabriela had become Gaby and had left to follow the road she'd once hoped Eli would travel with her. In retrospect, she realized he'd never once spoken of a shared future as he'd spurred her on.

With her father's silence ringing in her ears nearly as loudly as her longing for Eli, Gaby had left.

Gabriela Lucía Navarro had become, for all intents and purposes, an orphan.

Now it was official.

Gaby's body rocked in misery, her face scraping against the rough fabric she wouldn't let herself defile with much-too-late, useless tears. Finally, she rose, went into her room and undressed by the faint golden glow of one small lamp, then slid between the sheets.

She would bury her father tomorrow, but

his heart had been buried many years before, lost when her mother had died. When his dreams of a legacy had dried to dust at the hands of his ambitious daughter.

ELI FOCUSED THE CAMERA on the two men a couple of hundred yards away. Their body language was too relaxed; tonight there would be no delivery, but he would capture their faces to add to his collection of evidence.

He waited another hour, watching them smoke and murmur and grow somnolent, then he slipped away to make his rounds.

When he got to Gaby's house, he avoided the barn to prevent the horse from nickering in greeting. Tomorrow, during the funeral, he would check on Paco's feed and water, perhaps manage more than the cursory grooming he'd dared in daylight forays, since no one would be on the premises.

Frank Navarro had gambled by summoning the man he'd despised, and lost his life in the process. There was no one left to put things aright, no other person who could clear Eli and give him back his life.

He neared the house and made an unwarranted trip beneath her bedroom window, blaming curiosity.

Then the light flicked on.

Eli retreated into the shadows.

But he didn't leave. And when he heard her weeping, his hands clenched into fists.

Once she would have turned to him for comfort, light-years ago. Back when Gaby had made her innocent's view of the world seem sensible…and he, the wild boy who understood only the darker realities, had been too dazzled by the miracle of her to argue.

Everything in him tensed as he felt her grief roll over him, but with a discipline that had been years' in the making, he remained where he was.

Keeping vigil.

Untold moments passed, and Gaby's sobs slowed to the occasional sniffle. The light went out and he heard, through the open window, the intimate sounds of her body shifting on the mattress.

Eli remained motionless for a long time.

Then he resumed his nightly patrol.

THE FUNERAL MASS was a blur.

Facing these people she had once known

so well had required every ounce of strength Gaby possessed. Their compassion was almost worse than the accusations she felt floating in the air.

Only two people had stood out: Chad, who'd remained by her side every second. And Ramón, who'd taken her into his arms like a lost child.

She couldn't recall Ramón ever being young, but now he was ancient and bony. Frail, yet as kind as ever. A man of few words, eyes dark with sorrow. *"Dulcita."* *Sweet one,* his pet name for her. "I will help you with Paco tonight."

She hadn't spared a thought for her father's horse the night before. What would become of Paco when she left?

"No need. I'll be caring for Gabriela," Chad said.

The possessive tone grated on her. "I can do that for myself."

Chad's jaw tightened, and she regretted her rudeness. "Thank you both, however."

Ramón glanced between them, hugged her once more and murmured promises to assist her in any way he could, then backed away.

At the graveside, Gaby remained long

after everyone had left. Her eyes were dry; the body into which she hadn't been able to put any food felt as empty and brittle as cornstalks gone brown in harsh sun.

Her father's body had been reduced to mere ashes. She would never touch him again, never be held in those strong arms.

She could think of no words to say, no way to write an ending she could live with.

She swayed on her feet, and Chad's arms were around her in an instant. "That's it," he snapped. "I'm taking you to my place and putting you to bed."

His presumption stiffened her spine. She jerked from his grip. "I'm not your problem, Chad."

"Someone should be there for you, Gabriela. You're all alone now."

"I've been alone for years." She forced herself to soften the harshness of her response and placed one hand on his forearm. "Chad, I appreciate very much everything you've done. This—" she gestured around them with a trembling hand "—would have been so much more difficult without you. But you're sacrificing time from the search for my father's killer, and I can't let you do it anymore."

"My men can handle the hunt. I stay in constant contact."

"I'm sure you do, but you're wearing yourself out."

"I know my limits."

"You look exhausted. Take me home, then go get some rest."

"I have too much to do to—"

She nodded in satisfaction. "Just as I guessed." She let her weariness show. "I'll be fine. I'll make myself something to eat and then lie down." She squeezed the firm muscle beneath her hand. "I can't think anymore, Chad. It's all too overwhelming. Let's both get a good night's sleep, and we can talk tomorrow."

His reluctance was clear, but he didn't argue any longer. The trip back to the ranch was silent. Gaby jittered inside with the need to be alone.

She mustered the strength to bid a polite farewell and thank him again. Then, with relief, she watched the wheels of his big truck spin on the caliche as, she hoped, he went home to seek his own reprieve.

With one hand on the screen door, she prepared to go inside—

And felt the darkness within steal over her, smothering her with its thick blanket of desolation. Instead of doing as she'd promised, Gaby dropped her purse on the concrete porch and fled into her father's garden to tear at weeds.

If only it were as easy to rip out the haunting remnants of all she and her father would never have the chance to mend.

THE FLAMES ROARED HIGH, merciless maws of destruction consuming everything in their path. "No—Mom! No, I'm coming— Let me go—"

Eli jolted awake, heart pounding.

Doggy breath hit his nose just before the wide, wet tongue lapped upward across his cheek.

He coiled to defend. "What the…"

The cave. Not the house, not the barn.

And daylight outside.

A furry head butted against his leg. Another lick. A whimper.

"You okay?" He scanned the dog, noted nothing to alarm him. Scrubbed his face and recalled that he'd set his internal alarm clock for only four hours of sleep so that he could tend to the old man's horse while Gaby was gone to bury her father.

Gaby. Sobbing in her bed. Alone, as she shouldn't have been, if only he'd been able to act more quickly on her father's tip.

He let his head fall into his palms, then rose and stretched.

The dog wriggled with impatient glee. If the canine had had more than a stub of a tail on that boxer's body, he'd have thumped the wall in his eagerness.

"You are one ugly mutt, you know that?"

The dog just lowered his head to the ground, sniffing ardently around the edges of the cave. After checking to be sure there was still water in the animal's bowl, Eli topped it off, took a long drink for himself to empty one jug, then put that aside to replenish from the well at the homestead.

He grabbed some jerky and entertained visions of crawling right back in the pallet.

But the horse would be hungry, too.

And Eli was tired of being solely a creature of the night.

He laced up his boots, grabbed the jug and

strode outside. The dog shot past him, then slowed his pace long enough to hike his leg here and there. He scented the morning breeze and was off to the next bush to warn off any males foolish enough to trespass. He sniffed so loudly Eli could hear every snort.

He grinned. "That's the way, fella. Mark and conquer. We males have simple needs." He watched the animal race away on his first long jaunt since Eli had found him and admired how the dog was regaining strength.

The dog's head lifted suddenly.

"Hear that?" Eli listened to Paco's nicker coming from the barn. "You ever seen a horse, fella?" Patting his thigh, he signaled the dog to follow. The animal complied, trotting along at his side, tongue hanging out as he panted eagerly.

Eli chuckled. "If not, you're about to meet the biggest dog you ever laid eyes on."

But with every step nearer the homestead, he thought about hearing Gaby last night. For him to ignore someone so alone, someone in that much torment, went against the grain.

Eli entered the barn and snapped his attention back to the dog. He grabbed the collar he'd woven. How dogs and horses would react when they hadn't grown up together was unpredictable.

He approached the stall and crouched beside the canine, who quivered, then barked. The horse stirred.

"Easy, boy, he's behind a big old stall door. He can't hurt you."

The sorrel snuffled at the boards, shook his head and whinnied. The dog backed up.

"Pretty huge, huh?" Eli smiled at the hound, head low in submission as he approached the dreaded giant.

When the big sorrel stamped his feet, the dog raced back to Eli and whimpered.

Eli laughed. He approached the horse, palm out for the animal to scent.

The sorrel stepped back, then neared again, head lowered to sniff at Eli's hand.

"Yeah, you remember me, right?" He smoothed a stroke down the long nose, then patted his neck and smiled. The horse leaned closer, as if seeking comfort—or food, more likely. "Sorry, nothing on me right now."

He opened the stall door and strode inside, keeping one hand on the horse at all times. The dog hovered outside, but Eli focused on

Paco. He slipped a halter over Paco's head and led him out, tying him near the barn door so he could see the open spaces.

Eli grabbed a wheelbarrow, rake and shovel and cleaned out the stall, then filled the water trough and replenished the feed.

Next he moved to the tack room and selected a curry comb, a hoof pick and a brush. When he came back out, horse and dog seemed to have reached a truce. Paco ignored the dog, and the dog stayed out of Paco's way, perhaps instinctively understanding the danger of those hooves.

Eli placed the tools on a hay bale nearby. He chose to start with the curry comb, working out a few burrs and bits of mud that had collected in the horse's coat.

Paco shifted occasionally but remained impressively still. The dog finally settled and, with a deep exhalation, laid his head on his paws and shut his eyes.

Eli moved on to the hoof pick, talking quietly to the horse as he bent over each leg. Paco was not so sanguine about this stage, but he accepted Eli's touch fairly well. Once finished, Eli began brushing the horse's coat, and Paco grew so still he almost seemed asleep, his head lowered. The rhythmic motions and the scents soothed Eli, too. He listened to the horse's slow breaths and heard the birds chirping. The dog snored softly.

Eli couldn't recall the last time he'd felt this relaxed.

Then he heard the sound of an engine and knew time was up. He'd let himself lose track. He had to get out of there before his presence was discovered.

He returned Paco to his stall, then withdrew into the shadows of the barn to wait for his chance to escape.

When the big black Ford spun its tires on the caliche, Eli's lip curled at the sight of Chad Anderson.

Once the sheriff was gone, Eli approached the door. Poised to slip around to the side and make himself scarce, Eli nearly missed the slender figure in black, her frame a study in dejection.

Gaby. There she was, after nine long years.

Funny, when he should remember only her desertion, that apparently the boy who had loved her so foolishly and fully still lived inside him. Craved to see her face again, just one time.

Damn it.

He pulled the length of rope from his rear pocket and tied the dog to one slat of the nearest stall, murmuring the nightly order that had, thus far, kept the canine quiet and safe.

He wouldn't speak to her. There was nothing to say, anyhow. They'd been kids. He only wanted one good glimpse of her, then he would fade away as quickly as he'd come.

He eased through the barn door and made his way toward the woman who had once been the one bright light in his life.

CHAPTER THREE

HER SLENDER BACK WAS BOWED as he spotted her through the pale greenery of the few struggling tomato plants doomed to die when the first frost hit any day now. Her black dress was streaked with dirt; her sable hair glinted red in the sunlight.

Against the sound of the breeze, Eli heard the gurgle of the hose two rows over. Thirsty soil slowed the path of the restorative water, yet the dark ribbon lengthened, moment by moment.

Strong, graceful fingers struggled with a stubborn weed. Tears streamed, as though endless, down her face.

His heart clenched at the sight of the smooth, tawny curve of her jaw, glistening with its patina of sorrow. The moment was so private and filled with pain that he hesitated. Thought to disappear.

Yet, however much she'd betrayed what they'd once meant to each other, something within him balked at leaving her this alone.

The weed broke at the stalk, and she grappled for balance, crouched as she was on black high-heeled sandals. She stood up abruptly, her shiny dark hair swinging, the sleek curving ends barely kissing the slope of her shoulders.

The green stalk clutched in her hand oozed milky-white fluid from its torn body, and there was a tearing ache in those beautiful, haunting eyes. Despite all that had passed, he found himself wanting to pluck out her pain. Wished for the power to make those caramel eyes sparkle again.

To protect her.

Her body swayed to a dirge he could almost hear. To remain where he was required everything in him.

But when she began to crumple—

He bolted into action. Caught her before she fell. "Gaby—"

Her lids fluttered. "Eli?" The last of the color in her face drained away. Her body collapsed like a doll with the stuffing yanked out.

He swept her into his arms and made for

the house as the dying plant dropped from nerveless fingers. Once inside, he spared no time for a survey of the place he'd never been allowed to enter. Instead, he headed for the room he calculated to be the one she'd been in last night. He laid her out on the bed that clearly belonged to a young girl, elevated her feet, removed her shoes and loosened her clothing with fingers that were shaking.

He left her only long enough to pour water into a bowl and snag a cloth, then dipped it, wrung it out and stroked the cooling moisture over her skin.

Not until her color started to improve did he draw a steady breath. He placed a chair beside the bed and poised there, elbows on thighs, hands propping his chin.

He devoured the details of her appearance, this woman who had been formed from the raw clay of a naive, headstrong girl.

She was too thin.

He smiled at that; few women today believed such a state possible, but he remembered a girl who was more rounded. Softer. Optimistic and determined.

The face that had emerged was equally

intent. Prominent cheekbones, lashes as thick as ever, though elegant brows had been honed from ones he recalled as less structured. The chin that had jutted in his direction many a time was still ready to declare her independence.

And the mouth…oh, that glorious mouth, framed now by a face that was noble and proud.

Her dress, sleek and beautifully tailored, clung to a figure better left unnoticed.

As if that were possible. His fingers flexed with the urge to touch.

He reminded himself he'd always understood that she wasn't for him, even before the night she'd failed to show at their rendezvous spot. If she hadn't possessed such grand ambitions and the skills to accomplish them, he still would never have entangled her in the coil that was his life. Gaby was the light to his darkness, the ray of hope he'd never truly believed in.

But from the day she'd walked into his hospital room after she'd saved his life on a deserted country road, Eli's soul had belonged to her for as long as she'd wanted it. Others had had different plans for her, but for sweet, stolen months, they had shared a love that could only survive in the darkness…and for a time, he had forgotten that, sooner or later, daylight exposed everything the night disguised.

Gaby stirred. But she never fully rose to consciousness. Eli held his breath, as eager for her to awaken as he was praying she would not.

When she settled again, he filled the water glass on the bedside table and watched her a little longer. Checked her pulse and color once more.

Then, with quiet steps, he left.

Before temptation placed her life in danger. Again.

GABRIELA AWOKE IN HER childhood bed, the walls still covered with the tiny yellow rosebuds that had seen her through childhood and her first kiss. For a moment, she drank in the cool, clean air, the feeling of rightness.

And then she recollected the voice she'd heard. The blurred form.

Jolted up straight. "Eli?"

Only silence greeted her. She sat on the

edge of the double bed handed down from her grandmother, her head achy, her eyes tired from weeping. She longed to seek oblivion in sleep again.

She realized the buttons were opened at the neck of the dress she'd worn to her father's funeral. Spotted the water in the glass on the bedside table.

Could it possibly have been him? She drank in greedy gulps, then rolled her wrist inward. Tucked the glass against her chest as if she could capture the phantom who'd left it for her.

Eli was spotted right here, arguing with your father…. He'll be charged with your father's murder.

How to square the boy who'd loved her with the one suspected of his mother's death? The subject of a manhunt with a man who would put her to bed and leave her a glass of water?

Why had he returned?

She thought of the day, her junior year of high school, when she and Chad had encountered Eli on the side of the road, unconscious. They had hauled him to a doctor in Alpine, a hundred miles away, but Eli had refused to reveal who'd beaten him so badly, and he hadn't welcomed her interference as he'd begun to heal.

She'd persisted, however. His mother had had no car and had come only sporadically; no one else had bothered. Gaby had paid him daily visits until his release, when her father had found out and lowered the boom. He'd been no happier than Chad about her interest in the boy everyone had considered little better than a wild animal.

Then had commenced the sweetest months of her life. Meeting Eli in secret in the depths of night. Letting him show her the outdoors he'd learned to inhabit to escape life at home and horrors he would not explain.

He changed the topic every time she wanted to discuss why he chose to camp out rather than go home, why he attended school barely enough to pass and cared nothing at all about grades or achievement. He would listen for hours to her plans and her dreams, but he never revealed his.

Except one that shouted from his eyes without him ever saying a word: Eli wanted Gaby for his own.

But he would never claim her. Just the

opposite, in fact, no matter how hungry his gaze on her or how a fever shimmered in the air between them, Eli would not touch her beyond a kiss now and then.

Yet kisses she now understood as relatively chaste still shone more brightly in her memory than any she'd experienced since.

He was willing to teach her field craft and desert lore, would encourage even her highest aspirations, but he kept an iron grip on the urges raging inside him.

Too naive to realize how remarkable his control was for a teenage boy, she teased him without mercy, desperate to use any means possible, however untutored her efforts, to grasp on to a promise of a future he refused to envision. With all the passion of a young girl's heart, she painted dreams for him he would never claim. She invaded his physical space at every opportunity, sensing, untried as she was, the leverage she could gain to anchor him to her.

With each meeting, they edged closer to crossing that line, and she'd been certain that last night would be The One.

Instead, she was locked in her room by her

father, while Eli's mother was trapped inside another one that was burning.

And Gaby had never laid eyes on Eli again.

Until today.

She might have dreamed him. Chad could have been the one who'd put her to bed.

But even as she considered those options, she discarded them.

Not that it could matter. If Eli wanted her, he would have stayed. She had plenty to do. A house to pack up, memories to shed before she returned to New York.

If only she didn't feel a hundred years old.

Coffee was probably the worst choice when her stomach ached from everything trapped within her, but she managed to shower and dress, then padded toward the kitchen.

Every step of the way, a plan was forming. She could find him. She knew his haunts as no one else did.

But Chad was the sheriff. Eli was his business. She had an important job waiting, and she had to prove she could handle it.

In the kitchen, she drew another big glass of water while she waited for the coffee to percolate. She drank half without stopping, thinking that bottled water had never tasted nearly as good.

Her gaze skidded over the door to her father's room.

How much longer do you plan to delay? She hadn't yet been able to consider going inside, but she would have to deal with the room—with the whole house—if she was to get back to New York soon.

Just a peek, while the coffee's making. Squaring her shoulders, she walked down the hall and pushed the door open.

The old blue chenille bedspread her mother had loved still covered the bed, now threadbare in spots, the tufts worn off like the fur on Gaby's childhood teddy bear. She stared at the ceiling and swallowed back tears.

Too many memories.

Gripping the knob, she glanced around the room. Her father might have just walked out and would return any moment. She felt like an interloper.

In truth, that was all she was. A stranger who'd been in these rooms before. In another existence.

Her gaze halted at the corner altar he'd kept even after her mother had died. Gaby ventured one cautious step, then another.

The statue of the Virgin that had been passed down from her mother's mother stood beside the candle to Santa Lucía, Gaby's saint name. Draped over the Virgin was her mother's rosary. Even now, Gaby could recall the pride at helping her father pick it out. She had thought the glass beads, with their lavender glow, were the most beautiful things she'd ever seen—perfect for her stunning mother, gone so many years now that she no longer seemed real.

The same old wooden crucifix hung on the wall behind, the gilt all but powder. Plastic flowers nearby were laden with the same layer of dust covering every surface in this house. Her father had been neat by nature, but dirt was a constant problem in this dry country.

She blew off the thick film from the glass top—and faltered. Picture after picture, pressed between glass and table. Gaby with her mother. Gaby in second grade. At her confirmation. She strangled on the torrent of emotion.

Then she spotted the program from her college graduation, with her name as summa cum laude.

And ran from the room as though chased by demons.

He never answered my invitation. I had no idea whether he got it. I believed he didn't care. Shaken to her soul, Gaby dug nails into her arms to keep from screaming out her anger. Crying out her wrenching, terrible sadness. *Why wouldn't you tell me you were there? Would it have been so hard, Papa?*

I believed I could never come home.

Gasping from the effort to hold in the anguish, she forced herself away from the wall and into the kitchen to pour coffee. With steps she never registered, she found her way out to the porch. Made it to the top stair, set the cup of hot liquid down.

The salty sobs would be swallowed back no more. Oblivious to everything but the agony clawing to get out, Gaby dropped her head to her knees, rocked by agonizing surges of a grief too ugly to heal.

Then there was a snuffle at her ear.

A wet tongue on her arm.

Gaby recoiled. A big head nudged at her. A faint whine. Sad brown eyes.

"Where did you come from?"

Thin and scarred, the dog whimpered again.

She didn't really care; for that moment, her terrible loneliness eased. When he butted her hand gently for more petting, she even managed a tiny smile. She scratched behind his ears and rubbed her forehead against his as soft pants bathed her face.

Merely petting him quieted her turmoil. "I don't know where you came from, but thank you."

His only answer was a wag of his tail, but somehow he'd brought sunshine into her despair.

"I'm hungry. How about you? Want to go inside?" She rose and went to the door, waiting to discover if he'd go or stay, hoping desperately that he'd choose the latter.

To invite him in made no sense, as she would only be here a few days. She'd search for his owner before she left, though she doubted he had one. His ribs showed, and he bore the scars of recent injury.

Perhaps Ramón would help her locate a good home for him.

For now, though, she welcomed company that wouldn't ask questions or talk about the past.

After a moment's hesitation, he followed her.

And Gaby found her first honest smile since she'd picked up the phone in New York.

FROM A DISTANCE, Eli watched them.

But soon he turned away, weary from a fruitless night of searching, and left to make his way to the cave.

Alone.

CHAPTER FOUR

GABY MADE HERSELF breakfast from the pitiful contents of her father's refrigerator: a lone egg, a forlorn sliver of longhorn cheese, a withered onion. The half loaf of bread bore a faint blue shadow, so into the trash it went. She rummaged through the cabinets and found a packet of saltines that would have to suffice.

What she wouldn't give for a fresh tortilla.

She hardly ever cooked anymore, but all at once, she could feel the dough soft and giving beneath her hand. Could picture a ball of it lying on the bread board extending from its hiding place beneath the counter, the small rolling pin flattening, then spreading the dough until it was thin just this side of tearing. Could smell the nutty fragrance as it browned on the griddle.

She would make tortillas once, here in this kitchen where she had made hundreds.

Her own ceremony of parting, since she would never be back.

Having one concrete plan steadied her. She finished making the omelet and halved it to share with the dog. While she ate, she began a grocery list. Between bites, she checked the cabinets for flour and lard. Opened a drawer and felt the prick of tears at the sight of the rolling pin that had been her mother's and before her, Gaby's grandmother's.

"*Chica,*" she could hear her mother say, "someday you will teach your *niña*, and the line of women will link, past to future. That is what we do, our people. We plant our roots in the soil. We endure whatever life hands us and we go on."

Oh, Mama. In that moment, Gaby's mother, Celia, was alive again, small and curvy and fierce. *I can't stay. I'm sorry. I'm not like you, however much Papa wished for that.*

Gaby shoved away from the counter. The house closed in around her like a coffin. She would have withered here, but sometimes—

I have the life I wanted. I'm going to be someone to reckon with, Papa. Just you wait and—

But Papa would never see. She had been without family for several years, but now that state was permanent. Final.

She was completely alone.

For the first time since the tumult that had greeted her arrival, she registered the absence of her cell phone. In New York, it was her most constant accessory, seldom turned off. Her existence was contained in it, her calendar, all her contacts and what passed for her social life. She was hardly ever at home, if the hovel she inhabited could be termed as such.

Truth was, Gaby had no home now. She lived for her job; that was what a modern American woman did. What was required to succeed in the most exciting, ambitious city in the world.

What her father could never understand.

For a second, she could hear the bustle of Manhattan, the whoosh of bus air brakes, the roar of the subway trains below. Cab horns blaring. Sirens. The city was an unceasing roar, an omnipresent wall of noise that she'd thought at first would drive her mad, however much she'd longed for it.

Nowadays she scarcely noticed.

But here…the deep silence was a living thing, so complete that a single car's engine drew notice. A bird's lilt. If Manhattan was a sky roiling with thunderclouds and lightning, West Texas was night so dark and clear you could almost hear the stars hum.

The dog whined, and Gaby snapped back into the present.

The grocery list lay beneath a hand gone slack, so relaxed had she become in the stillness.

List. Right. She rubbed between her eyes with her middle finger.

Flour. Dog food.

She glanced at the animal sitting so quietly and holding her in his steady gaze. "What brand do you like, boy?"

He cocked his head, and she could imagine his snort. As thin as he was, being picky about food was a ridiculous notion.

Nearly as absurd as acquiring a dependent when she couldn't wait to get away. A commitment to him would only slow her down. Perhaps, however, when she returned to New York, she'd start looking at apartments that allowed pets.

That idea had her glancing toward her new

tenant, now occupied in sniffing his way around the kitchen. "What do you think, pal? Want to become a big-city dog?"

He walked to the screened back door, looked out and whimpered.

"I guess not." She stood behind him, her gaze drawn to the endless vista. "With all this to roam, why would you accept spending every day in a small apartment?"

Why do you? asked a voice she couldn't identify.

With a jolt, she realized how far away New York seemed, and the thought had her spinning from the door in panic.

The dog whined again.

"Just a minute," she muttered, rummaging a little desperately through her purse. "Got it," she crowed.

She powered up her cell and retraced her steps, then opened the screen door. The dog bounded outside. Gaby followed but paid no attention to his path, too intent on waiting for the signal strength indicator to appear.

"Damn." *One bar, please. Just one little—*

She circled in a slow spin, alert for any improvement. *Come on, come on—*

"Yes!" Jubilantly, she hit her speed dial,

mentally calculating the time difference, sure that Beth, the early riser, would already be in the office—

"You have reached the offices of *Bijou* magazine. Our hours are—"

What? Where were—

Then it hit her. This was Sunday morning. Even the most driven staff members wouldn't be in; even she, who practically lived at the office, went there seldom on Sundays and then, not until afternoon.

She dialed her boss's extension. Listened to the message like a lifeline to the real world.

Her boss's voice was real. Gaby's life there was real. She would return; she wouldn't get swallowed up by Chamizal. The past had no power to harm her now.

But when the beep sounded, what rose to her lips was absurdly emotional, nothing like the Gaby everyone knew. She had developed cunning and armor a young, lovesick girl had never imagined needing.

Right now, though, the words poised to spill from her throat were nothing like the woman she'd become.

So she settled for "Hi, it's Gaby. Just

checking in. I'll—" *Be on the next plane,* she wanted to say.

Even more, however, she yearned to rid herself of this place and its ghosts once and for all, and that would require a few days to clear up her father's estate, however pitiful it was. "The funeral is over, but there are details to finalize." A hitch in her voice had her biting her lip. She cleared her throat and resumed speaking as the Gaby she'd become, crisp and efficient. "I'll get on it first thing tomorrow and notify you in a day or two when I'll be back."

She ended the call. Clutched the cell to her breast and stared toward the horizon, but what she was visualizing was Forty-second Street, midtown Manhattan. The view from the corner office windows that might someday be hers.

A nicker from the barn snapped her reverie. The dog sat in front of her, tongue lolling.

Did it really matter whether she visited Paco or not? Ramón could care for him until she found him a good home. Ditto the dog at her feet. Did she honestly have to take any more steps into the quicksand of her past by facing the animal that was the last living reminder of her father?

Gut it up, Gaby. Nothing in Chamizal can match what you tangle with every day in New York.

But Paco wasn't the only memory lying in wait in the barn, nor was Papa. She and Eli had met there in secret on nights when the weather was too bad to rendezvous outdoors.

Just his name rattled her.

He hated your dad for coming between you.

How could Chad know that? She'd never seen Eli again after her father had locked her in her room and forbidden her to see him. Eli had disappeared that same night.

He had never been a creature of hate with her. Prickly with the world, yes. Troubled and solitary and a little like the dog before her, rail thin and hungry far beyond any need for food.

He'll be charged with your father's murder.

Where are you, Eli? To believe him guilty of her father's murder or his mother's death would mean that he'd changed drastically from the boy she'd known. Loved.

But you've *changed.* She had. A lot. Maybe Eli...

She squeezed her eyes shut and shook her head. She had a life to go back to; she couldn't get involved with his.

And her father was dead. However it had happened, he was gone. What did it matter why? It was too late to seek his forgiveness, to make peace between them, to tell him how much she—

Loved him. *Oh, Papa...*

Gaby resisted the urge to sink to the ground, enervated by her grief, by all the loose ends whipping around in the gale-force winds of her past, tearing at her hair and scratching her face. There was no peace to be found here, and if she lingered, she would be sucked back into everything she had fought so hard to escape.

She eyed the back door and longed to go inside, pack her one suitcase and get the hell out of Dodge.

But first, she had to find the truck keys. And however badly she wished to flee, undoubtedly there was a hungry animal in the barn. She could at least turn him out into the pasture, where he could graze on his own and obtain water from the stock tank until Ramón made it over to care for him.

Like a prisoner facing execution, she headed for the barn.

Once inside the cool, dim interior, Gaby paused to let her eyes adjust. At the far end, sunlight beckoned.

Nothing had changed. But everything had.

A hundred scenes played out in her mind: Papa beaming as she clutched the reins for her first, breath-stealing ride alone on Honey. Papa had rescued the mare from old man Rodriguez's heavy hand, bartering two precious calves from his herd for his horse-mad daughter, despite the reality that only a working horse was practical on a struggling ranch.

But it had been her first birthday without her mother, and a milestone one, at that. Thirteen and left with no female relatives, only a father reeling from his own grief and scarcely managing to survive dealing with her first menstrual period just one month earlier.

Celia Navarro would have made a pretty cake and concocted a party with appropriate flourishes; Frank Navarro was out of his depth in the female domain. He had left Gabriela's rearing to her mother; he would assume the lead with a son. But instead of sons, Celia had miscarriages. She'd kept trying until her body had weakened. An ordinary flu had turned into pneumonia, and she was gone.

Taking the heart of their home with her.

A welcoming whicker from the far end of the barn dragged Gaby back to the present.

"Hey, boy." She found her way to the stall. Paco stuck his head over the rail, and automatically, she began to pet him, scanning his form for signs of neglect.

When she didn't spot them, she unlatched the door and stepped inside. "Are you hungry? I'll grab a bucket and—"

She frowned. His feed bucket was nearly full, and the water in his trough was free of debris. She walked around him and noted the shine to his coat. Picked up a hoof and saw that it was well maintained. "Ramón's been here already, has he?" As she stroked the horse, he nudged his big head into her side. She couldn't help smiling. "I'm glad he's tending you, but I guess you're still lonely, huh?" She rested her forehead against his withers.

"Me, too," she whispered.

Then the tears she'd been fighting off would be stifled no longer.

Paco stood still while she cried. Her father was everywhere, but nowhere more than with this companion he had loved. Paco had been a working horse when she'd left, a fine, strong animal capable of herding cattle and bracing to pull a stump from the ground, of enduring hot summer days and bearing a calf over his hindquarters.

Gaby had always suspected that even if Paco had not been as hard a worker as the man who'd owned him, her father still would have moved heaven and earth to keep him, hay burner though any horse was.

Now Paco was old, and his master was dead. Gaby grieved for how his life would change when, inevitably, she must send him away.

Paco nudged her again, and blew across her arm as if entreating her to play.

Gaby scraped at her wet cheeks. "How long since you've had a good run, boy?" She glanced down at the slim, tailored slacks she'd donned. Perfect for city streets but all wrong here.

If she wasn't mistaken, nothing in her room had been changed. A pair of her old jeans might still be in the drawers.

For the second time that morning, a beast brought her the grace of a smile. "You wait right here. I'll be back."

ELI COULDN'T SLEEP, despite his exhaustion. The cave was cool and quiet, but he was newly aware of just how long it had been since he'd slept in a real bed. Had a meal at a table. Moved around in the light without wondering who might spot him.

Not for the first time, he considered walking away. He had no real stake here. Whatever small connection he'd had with Chamizal had ended nine years ago, with his mother's death.

With Gaby's abandonment.

Damn it. He shoved away the sleeping bag, rose to his feet. Stalked to the cave mouth and stared across the expanse of dun and gray-green. The longing to wrap up his half-assed investigation gnawed at his gut, the desire to be anywhere but Chamizal stronger yet. If only Gaby—

There the problem lay. Gaby was here,

like it or not, and as long as she was, he was bound to stay. No one was aware of his oath except a dead man; he could leave with no one the wiser. Things would proceed as they had for years. No one but him cared.

Yet there was the rub. He had cared very much once, and he had made a promise.

To a man who had been murdered.

He could go back to his life as an Internet reporter, filing his daily dispatches under his pseudonym, Max Sager, at *The Hot Spot Journal,* from the far reaches of the planet. Crisscross from Bangladesh to Antarctica, Siberia to Morocco and stay out of the country indefinitely, as he had before Frank Navarro's message had arrived. There was nothing to tie him to the fire that had killed Frank.

The truth had stopped no one nine years ago, however. The cloud of suspicion would not disperse until he came up with proof.

He would depart again, but not yet, and when he left this time, it would be on his own terms. Gaby's presence was a complication; surely she would go back to New York very soon. Until she did, he must protect her, but once she left, he was free to resolve things in his own time. He could hide out here forever; he'd learned well when he was very young.

Resolve, however, did nothing to still restlessness. Gaby was too near and unaware of her danger. If she stayed only a day or two more, she would be all right. No one would harm her if she simply sold out.

Movement in the distance caught his attention. He squinted to make out the figure on horseback. When he realized who it was, first he swore. Then he smiled.

Then he simply watched in wonder as a stranger metamorphosed into a sight he hadn't witnessed in years.

Damn you, Gaby. Please. Go away.

I don't want to remember that girl anymore.

GABY HAD WALKED PACO first. He was not a young horse, and he'd been in the stall for at least a few days, she imagined. She was a runner and understood the value of stretches and warming up muscles.

She caught an eagerness in him, a touch of impatience, so she moved him to a trot. When he still strained at the bit, she let him out into full gallop. Across the acres, they flew, and Gaby found herself smiling.

When a form appeared off Paco's left flank, recognizing it as the dog required a second.

Then she began laughing for sheer joy.

The wind whipped hair she should have tied back if she'd been thinking, but thinking was the last thing she wished to do just now. Her thigh muscles burned with the unaccustomed exertion; her eyes teared from the wind—

None of that mattered. She was free at that instant, unencumbered by the past or the future for a few precious moments, and her spirits expanded to meet the endless blue sky above.

They raced, she and Paco, as though borne on the wings of morning, and in that span of time, he was not an old horse soon to be abandoned and she was not a woman with tenuous ties to a painful past.

They flew as if one being, and Gaby glimpsed a vision that promised she would get past this and put West Texas behind her forever. If that shutter-snap left her feeling bereft, she put it off to the occasion.

She was meant for much more than this desolate country could ever deliver. Her life brimmed with challenging work and fascinating people and untold heights to scale.

Those considerations were for later, though. Right now, she and Paco would run. "You okay, boy?"

He seemed to catch her intent and lengthened his stride even more.

Delight bubbled from her throat again.

SHE MADE QUITE A PICTURE, Eli mused, dark hair streaming behind her, lithe body arrayed over the horse's back. Gaby's profile had never been girlish, too bold and dramatic to fall easily into the category of cute.

Cute she was not, or even conventionally pretty. Arresting, yes. All woman and stop-your-heart beautiful now.

After a long, noisy bout of slurping, the dog returned to his side, still panting.

"Wear you out, boy?" Eli bent and scratched behind the dog's ears. "Go on and eat." He gestured toward the rear of the cave, where the animal slept not far from his bedroll.

The dog remained.

"Already fed you, did she?" Eli spoke

without removing his gaze from the figure receding into the distance. "Shouldn't be surprised," he murmured. "She always had a big heart."

Then, farther out, Eli spotted another figure moving northward in a track that would cross Gaby's path at the boundary dividing Navarro property from Anderson.

When recognition struck, he swore beneath his breath.

Stay away from her, he commanded silently. Eli might have no desire to claim her, but he'd dispatch his enemy to hell before he'd let him do it.

THE FENCE LINE HOVE INTO sight, and with it a mounted figure. Gaby pulled gently but steadily on the reins.

The cheer from the ride remained on her features. "Good morning, Chad."

"You are a sight for sore eyes, Gabriela."

The admiration in his expression only added to her pleasure. "Why, thank you, neighbor." Her lashes fluttered with her best Southern belle imitation.

Chad grinned. "It's good to see you smiling."

She wanted to cling to the optimism, not descend into mourning again. She wasn't naive enough to think she wouldn't still be forced to contend with it.

But not just yet.

"It's a welcome sensation."

"Had coffee yet? Or breakfast? María would love to cook for you. She's already asked me when the *niña* will be by to visit."

"María's still there?" Chad's father's housekeeper had been with them since Chad was in grade school and his parents had divorced. His restless, beautiful mother had left him with his dad and gone on to seek a more exciting life than that of a rancher.

He tipped his Stetson back and nodded. "She'll outlive me—I feel certain. She's always complaining because I don't settle down and provide her grandbabies to spoil. I've attempted to retire her, but she refuses to go. Says I can't do without her. Would waste away without her cooking." He patted a flat belly. "María never heard of low-carb cooking. I grab salads for lunch, but the pounds are always lurking."

From a purely feminine perspective, he was an undeniably handsome man in his prime. "You're managing fine, as far as I can tell."

His eyebrows waggled. "That mean you'll ride home with me?"

She started to ask, *For what?* but resisted the temptation of images swirling in her head. Chad had been a good kisser, as she recalled. He might very well be a good lover, too. He'd given plenty of signs already that he was willing.

She thought about how long it had been since she'd last enjoyed a good bout of sweaty sex. Too long, she realized. She'd been caught up in the battle to succeed and had channeled all her energies into that.

She cocked her head. "I might. But only for breakfast," she stipulated. Then relented a bit. "For now, anyway." If he was on board with the notion of simple physical release, they could perhaps arrive at an arrangement.

He nodded. "I'll settle for that for the moment." He winked. "And work on bringing you around over *migas*."

"*Migas*." She sighed at the mere notion of the spicy mélange of eggs and peppers, tortillas, onions, cheese and tomatoes. She'd worked off that scant excuse for an omelet already. "You drive a hard bargain."

He chuckled. "You ain't seen nothin' yet. Race you to the gate—" He was off like a shot.

"Come on, Paco." She glanced around her for the dog, but he had vanished. She shrugged, bent low in the saddle and nudged her heels into the horse's side. "Let's show the man what we're made of."

CHAPTER FIVE

ELI ROUSED AT THE DOG'S whimper, then fell back onto his sleeping bag with a groan. The sun was high in the sky, he could tell, even this far back in the cave. Near noon, most likely, so he'd only slept a couple of hours after Gaby had disappeared with Chad.

Fatigue had taken up permanent residence in his bones, and that was dangerous. The past several years as he'd traveled with his laptop and digital cameras to document events all over the globe, he'd mastered the art of sleeping wherever fate granted him the chance, dropping off instantly and waking quickly when emergency threatened.

But here, where at last he might be able to clear himself and set old ghosts to rest, he seemed to have lost the knack.

Since Gaby's arrival, that is.

For a moment, he let his mind wander to a place he'd avoided for years: the secret world he and Gaby had inhabited when they were young and believed in magic. Even he, who'd known too much of life's dark corners, had behaved in a manner that was innocent, redeemed and cleansed by the love of a girl who, despite losing her mother, had remained untouched in her faith in man's innate goodness.

If others had been aware of the time he and Gaby spent together, his reputation would have led to the inevitable conclusion that their activities were the sort of thing one expected of the bastard son of a kept woman.

Sheriff Anderson's kept woman, to be exact, though Eli hadn't understood the relationship between his mother and Chad's father when he'd been very young.

He had no idea if Chad was aware of it. Whether Chad had a clue what kind of man his father really was.

When Eli had made a kid's mistake and tried to use what he'd uncovered about the former sheriff's less savory enterprises as leverage to get the sheriff to leave Eli's mother alone, Bill Anderson had merely laughed, then told Eli that his mother was involved in them, too. He'd warned Eli that no one would suspect an officer of the law but that he would make certain Eli's mother went to jail if Eli breathed a word. He'd had one of his cohorts beat Eli so severely that Eli, abandoned on a deserted road, would have died had Gaby and Chad not happened upon him. Gaby barely knew him, yet she'd refused to leave his side until he'd received medical care.

While he'd been in the hospital, Gaby had shown up to check on the boy most regarded as little more than a wild animal. Something had stirred to life between them.

And the rest, as is said, was history.

Eli never revealed who had injured him, but his mother had surmised the truth and begged him to leave. She'd been trapped, and she'd desperately wanted her son away and safe. Eli had refused to abandon her, but he'd spent more and more time alone in the desert, watching over his mother and spying on the sheriff, looking for the man's Achilles' heel.

And meeting Gaby in secret.

Eli had been cognizant of what people thought about him, so however much he'd burned for Gaby, had longed to love her with his body as he had with his heart, he hadn't acted on it. He'd suffered, yes—the tortures of the damned—after he'd left her each time.

But with her, he'd been a kid again, he who'd left childhood behind early. They'd talked, they'd played…and sometimes he'd let himself believe they could have plenty of time to find the solution that would give them a future.

Eli could almost laugh at the boy who'd briefly become a romantic. The world was not an innocent place, nor was it a venue for dreamers. He'd learned that when he was too young, and his travels had reinforced the lesson.

He flopped over and beat down the poor excuse for a pillow, ordering himself to sleep, for the night ahead of him was full.

Then he heard the dog whine and roused.

Just in time to see Gaby and Paco race past in the distance, as though the hounds of hell were after her.

The dog glanced at him, then toward Gaby and back to him once again.

"Go on, boy. It's okay. Maybe she needs you."

The clap of his hands seemed to release the animal from his dilemma. With a spring of coiled muscle, after Gaby he went.

While Eli watched.

And despite everything, he couldn't help but regret all they had lost.

GABY DISMOUNTED FROM PACO and led him into his stall. She reached for the saddle her father had cherished, but when she'd uncinched it, she pauscd and traced one finger over the elaborate tooling.

Frank Navarro had been a proud man and for good reason, however little she'd understood it. He'd once been a vaquero of no small renown, to hear Celia tell the story. Gaby could dimly recall her mother's shining eyes as she reminisced about the handsome young man who had swaggered into her life and won her heart.

The saddle, a prize in a rodeo held across the border, was all that remained of his glory days. Gaby had never been able to connect her mother's tales to the work-worn man who'd struggled to keep his ranch, and his hopes for it alive.

Do as our fathers had planned, Chad had

said. Gaby doubted that Bill Anderson had possessed the same vision as her father, but she'd only known Chad's sire as a distant, forbidding figure.

Combining their ranches so that Gaby's husband could tend the land her children would inherit was the only legacy Frank Navarro had hoped to wrest from the ashes of his wife's death.

Chad was a nice man. He'd already gone out of his way to be kind to her, and he was willing to do more—much more, if she read his expression correctly.

Would it be so bad to simply spend a little time with him and let her heartache and grief settle? She was tired, so tired, and it wasn't only this place or losing her father. She hadn't taken any vacation in two years, relentlessly focused on her climb. She often worked at home on weekends, as well as late into the night.

But her new position was waiting. However unreal it felt.

She let Paco's last hoof settle to the ground and switched to the curry comb. Long strokes served to soothe not only the horse but herself, and the silence, broken only by the wind and the occasional bird trill or insect buzz, uncoiled something too tightly wound inside her.

New York seemed treacherously far away, in this instant, and the thought unnerved her. She couldn't afford to lose her edge, or—

Or what, Gabriela? You'd wind up alone and friendless? Except for Beth, she practically was.

Just then, the dog trotted up and nudged at her leg. She scratched his ears and stared into the distance.

Paco swung his head around and butted her hand, seeking his share of attention.

The dog tensed but didn't leave her side, and soon she had both hands occupied. She smiled. Maybe she was a little short on friends of the human persuasion, but she had her own fan club.

Chad was not interested in mere friendship, she was all but certain. Still, they might reach a compromise.

Eli had once been dear to her, however painful his desertion. Perhaps she'd hallucinated him, but if not…this might be her chance to find out why he'd left her. Close that chapter of her life for good.

Her boss had offered her two weeks, while she'd insisted she'd be back in two days. Maybe she'd been wrong.

"Okay, boys," she said, giving them one last pat. "After I get you both fed and watered, it's time for a call to New York."

"WON'T YOU COME IN?" she asked the still-nameless dog a while later. "You did before."

He remained on the front porch, whined, but wouldn't enter.

She opened the screen door and bent to pick up the water dish. "Here. If I take your water in, will you follow?" She went ahead, but he didn't budge.

Neither did he leave, however. If she had any food with which to tempt him…

The remaining bits of a box of stale crackers she'd unearthed and smeared with the margarine she'd scraped off its paper wrapping hadn't done the trick. Not that she blamed him. Based on what she'd found, her father's eating habits had been abysmal.

If you'd still been cooking for him…

"No." Gaby uttered her refusal. She'd barely managed her conversation with Beth free of tears; her only hope to avoid them now, facing the prospect of weeding through her father's belongings, was to treat this as merely another project to be accomplished. No treacherous detours down memory lane. No *what-ifs*.

"You've made your bed, Gabriela. Deal with it."

Thus, she left the dog to what he appeared to view as guard duty, though she found herself musing over possible names for him.

Duke. There was something slightly noble about him, wasn't there?

She had to smile at herself. No, he wasn't the least regal—but there was the John Wayne aspect of him.

Okay, how about Butch? Well, he was definitely macho, not a soft and cuddly type, though he did relish being petted.

When he wanted it, at least. Not necessarily on anyone else's schedule.

A loner, then. Strong and…sad.

An Eli.

She was lost for endless seconds, mindful of the teenager who was now fully a man who had never had the chance to be a boy. He'd let her be silly with him and had come as close to playfulness with her as she imagined he'd ever allowed himself.

But there had always been a solemnity about Eli. A sorrow that hung over him, one he would not discuss. Their stolen hours had been replete with kisses she'd sighed over for days, with her head full of visions of a future as unlimited as the sky above. When the kisses had progressed into caresses, Eli had been the one who kept them from becoming more. Left to her, she and Eli would have lost their virginity to each other early on, but he, sensitive about being illegitimate, had refused to risk creating a child who would share the same fate, despite all her offers to obtain birth control that would free them from the worry. Condoms could break, he said, and if she sought out pills, the news would whip through Chamizal like a whirlwind.

They would wait, he insisted, as proper couples had managed to do for many generations before this era of easy sex that meant nothing.

She meant everything to him, he'd said, and refused to budge on the topic, however painful the yearning of their bodies.

Agonizing it had been, yet she would not relinquish one single second of the torture, because not being with Eli would have been much worse. As it was, they were lucky to be with each other one night every couple of weeks. She had tried to walk by his side at school, and he had threatened to drop out if she did. Theirs was a love that could be acknowledged only when they were away from others, he'd made very clear. She'd argued and pleaded and threatened, but he'd held firm. "You can't understand, Gaby," he'd told her over and over. "And I can't explain. Either you trust me or you don't."

She'd even broken things off between them once, hoping to force him to choose her over his dogged principles.

It had been the most miserable month of her life.

Finally, she'd slipped him a note in school, asking him to meet her that night, and when she'd seen him, so gaunt and troubled, she'd realized that the separation had been hard on him, too. The vulnerability in his eyes, at war with the resolute set of his jaw, kept her from demanding, yet again, an explanation.

Whatever he needed her to be, she would. What secrets he must maintain, she'd no longer push him to reveal. She'd matured a little during those endless days, forced to accept that love—and she did love him, desperately—was not black and white, nor was it as simple as she'd envisioned it.

And when, in the strained and ponderous silence of their reunion, she'd simply opened her arms to him, Eli had cried. Tears, from the most self-contained person she'd ever met to this day, had rattled her as she'd believed nothing else ever could. He'd been shaken, too, and it was then that he'd given in to his longings, and they'd laid their plans to run away together after graduation.

And only a month later, she'd lost him forever.

Gaby came to herself in her room, one hand on the knob of the drawer in which she'd hidden the meager store of souvenirs she had of Eli. She paused, afraid to check inside.

Several deep, calming inhalations later, she thought she was ready. She was a woman now, not the girl who'd been so lovesick over a boy who had abandoned her. She would never accept that he had killed his mother, but the truth was that he'd never used their fallback meeting place or the letter drop they'd set up, just in case their original plans didn't work out. Eli, reckless in the eyes of town residents, was, when he really cared, cautious to the extreme. He would not have trusted their plans to chance.

Thus, when he didn't show as scheduled and left no word for her, though she'd checked every day until she'd departed for college, Gaby had realized she would never see Eli Wolverton again. He had reverted to the wild boy and had run, both from a town too quick to judge him—

And from her, the girl who, in the end, couldn't convince him that she, alone of everyone he'd known, would not let him down. She was mature now and understood how unlikely their bond had been. How unsuited they were.

But he had to have been aware of how much his leaving abruptly would hurt her, and that put her convictions about how they'd felt for each other in question.

Gaby dropped her fingers from the drawer pull and stepped back before she committed an act of sheer folly. She was not that girl anymore, soft eyed and dreamy. He'd broken her heart once, and, with concerted effort, she'd covered the raw edges and gone on with her life.

Whoever Eli was now, the Gaby he'd loved did not exist.

With determined steps, she strode through the house, snagging her purse and the keys to her father's truck. All she would allow on her mind for the next couple of hours would be groceries.

"Come with me, boy." She snapped her fingers and held the truck door open while she waited to find out what he would do.

With a sheepish look, he bounded off into the distance.

"I'll still buy you some dog food," she shouted after him. "And Eli couldn't be a more appropriate name—but I'm calling you Buddy. Because I could really use one."

CHAPTER SIX

WHERE WAS A GOURMET DELI when you needed it? Or even a simple corner Korean market? If you wanted a fully stocked grocery in this part of the world, you had to go to Alpine, and even then, you only had one option. Gaby shuddered at the mere notion of negotiating a superstore just now.

Cabrera's Grocery, right in Chamizal, was all she could manage. The basics were sold there; the only problem was the antagonism she would encounter. A good daughter took care of her *papi*. She'd abandoned her own. Whatever blame Frank Navarro bore for the tenor of their parting, she had been an adult for some time. She could have reached out to him instead of waiting for him to unbend.

But he had, hadn't he? Attended her college graduation, as evidenced by the program he'd kept.

Why, Papa? Why didn't you find me? Tell me I was forgiven?

Surely that was the meaning of all the clippings—that he hadn't disowned her after all. But whatever his reason, he hadn't made her aware of his presence, and she'd spent years without him when things could have been different.

She, just as much as he, shouldered responsibility for that. She emerged from the pickup, squared her shoulders and walked inside. Whatever blame she must face, it was justified.

The first instant was an assault of memory. Old Señora Cabrera ruling the cash register, her hair never permitted to stray from its original ebony, however great the contrast between aged skin and too-black hair, sweeping her relentless gaze up and down the six aisles whenever a child ventured in without parents, a common occurrence on hot summer afternoons after chores were completed. Gaby herself had raced there on dusty bare feet many a time, sent by her mother or, later, as the motherless child now in charge of Celia's kitchen herself.

Many days back then, her father had hardly paused in his working to eat, and even then, he'd tasted nothing, simply shoveled it in to provide fuel for the backbreaking task of keeping the ranch running. His escape from grief had been in his work. Gaby's had arrived in the form of books. For a while after her mother's death, Gaby had attempted to keep the house in the manner her mother had, all the homey touches, the good meals, the spotless floors.

She'd realized all too soon that her father noticed none of her effort, so gradually she'd reverted to simply handling the most pressing matters, getting laundry done and meals on the table. Every other hour that endless summer had been spent retreating into fiction. The bookmobile had come only twice a month; the librarian had taken pity on Gaby and authorized her to exceed the six-book limit, even turned a blind eye when Gaby delved into the adult-fiction shelves, save only the most clearly unsuitable material.

"Gabriela," said a voice from the past.

Gaby swiveled her head toward the sound. Blinked. "Linda? What are you doing here?"

Her girlhood friend, Linda Cabrera, now round with child, strolled across ancient, scarred wood floors toward her. "I live here."

"But—" Linda had had her own dream of becoming a clothing designer. She had dressed Gaby's dolls and her own, then graduated to making their prom gowns. After high school, Linda had been set to attend Texas Tech on a scholarship.

Linda smiled and stroked her belly. "Things change. I married Hank the summer after my freshman year. This is Cabrera-Latham number four."

"*Four* children?" Gaby blurted.

A line appeared between Linda's brows. "I love having babies. Raising children may not rate high in the big-city scheme, but it's important to us peons. It's the way we shape the future, by the values we teach them."

The defensiveness in Linda's tone had Gaby lifting her palms. "Of course it's important. I was just…surprised."

"I had them with me at the funeral mass."

She had registered nothing but a blur of faces. "I'm sorry. I was—"

Linda crossed the distance between them. "No, I'm the one who should apologize. Of course you don't remember. You were in shock. We all were." She laid one hand on Gaby's forearm. "Your father was a good man. He stayed to himself, but he was never unkind, just—" Linda fell quiet.

Gaby could too easily complete the sentence. "Lonely. Because his no-good daughter had abandoned him," she said bitterly.

"Don't, Gabriela. He never said that. He was...proud of you."

"Oh, great," Gaby said, pulling from Linda's grasp. "Rub it in, why don't you. I wasn't here when he needed me." Driving to Alpine suddenly didn't seem so bad.

"None of us was." Linda's voice held its own regrets. "No one expected this. I had no idea Eli was in town."

"Eli? Why do you bring him up?"

Linda flushed. "I— It's just that—"

"Tried and convicted him already just like Chad, have you? Does the whole town feel that way?"

"Gabriela, I heard the rumors, but I didn't want to credit them. You and Eli withheld quite a secret, didn't you? He had plenty of reason to hate your father, and there was his mother's death." Linda shook her head slowly. "Two fires…"

"I don't believe he would do such a thing," Gaby insisted. "He was always adopting injured animals and healing them. He loved his mother—I'm sure of it."

"Then why was he seldom at home? I can understand being embarrassed by her reputation, by how she barely kept him in clothes and most of those secondhand or patched, but he acted as if he hated her."

"When? Did you ever bother to get to know him? Did anyone?"

Eli might have left her without a word, but she couldn't bear to hear him so readily blamed. No one had ever understood him the way she had.

The way she *thought* she had, she amended. What was she really certain of except what he had permitted her to see?

"He didn't let people get close to him. He didn't even talk to you at school, for heaven's sake. What on earth did you see in him, Gabriela?"

A boy who had never learned to play, she nearly answered. *A heart that begged for care.*

But Gaby was abruptly too tired to discuss

Eli with anyone. A night spent tossing and turning was catching up to her. "I'm just here to pick up a few things, Linda."

Linda arched one eyebrow but gestured to the shelves. "Most items are exactly where they always were." Her tone was stiff with injury.

"Thank you." It was the best Gaby could do right now. For a second, she paused. Glanced back. "And thank you for attending Papa's funeral." Linda's expression didn't ease, so Gaby forced herself to make an effort. "Have you been told if you're having a boy or a girl?"

"We don't like to find out ahead of time. We enjoy the surprise. Our children are God's gifts, whatever the sex."

So it would be like this, strangers now. Gaby made her way to shelves stacked with the essentials of the mixed culture that was Chamizal—potato chips and saints' candles, white bread and *ristras* of peppers. Hers were random selections, not bothering with her grocery list. Dog food, she remembered, but otherwise she walked the aisles by rote and filled her basket. On impulse, she

bought a candle for the Virgin of Guadalupe, her mother's favorite.

Rounding one corner, she halted before a
display of tiny sugar skulls and abruptly
recalled that *Día de los Muertos* was just
over a month away.

The Day of the Dead, a long-standing cele-
bration dating back to pre-Columbian days,
was held on November second. It had, over
time, blended indigenous and Catholic
customs of All Saints' Day on November first
and All Souls' Day on November second.
Deceased loved ones were honored in a tradition that included building altars featuring
a photo of the loved one along with his
favorite foods and items. Families gathered at
the cemetery in a party atmosphere, both
paying homage to their dear departed and
inviting them to join the living for a day of fun.

Marigolds, or *cempasúchil*, from the
Nahuatl word *cempoalxóchitl*, were the
flower of the dead and appeared everywhere.
Likewise, skeletons were a part of the deco-
rations. Certain foods were traditional, such
as *pan de muerto* and *mole*. Soap was fre-
quently displayed in each collection because
the journey home was dirty.

Gaby had created her own altar to her mother the first year, but her grief-stricken father had refused to contribute, to even acknowledge it, much less have a party. She had lost heart and never done one again, but now, she couldn't stop her fingers from stretching out, cupping one sugar skull tenderly. Lifting it over her basket.

Would Papa's spirit even attend the party if she held one for him? Gaby couldn't be sure. She would be in New York by then, anyway. She started to set the skull back on the shelf, but in the end, she couldn't. Perhaps Papa wouldn't attend, but Mama might.

There would be places in Manhattan to find *Día de los Muertos* items—the city was a stew of cultures and there were many, many Latinos. This skull would not survive the flight home.

Still, she cradled it in her hand as she strode to the register.

Linda glanced at the skull and up to Gaby's face. For an instant, it seemed that they might connect.

Someone entered the store, and the moment was broken. Linda checked her out in silence, but when it came time to pay and Gaby proffered her credit card, her former friend merely shook her head and held out the book that had been used at Cabrera's since long before either of them was born. Gaby signed the ledger page reserved for Frank Navarro and noted the unpaid balance. At her first opportunity, she would have money wired to the bank in Alpine and make a trip to Cabrera's to pay them in cash.

One more reminder of affairs she must settle to get on with her life.

"Goodbye," she said to Linda at the door.

"Come back soon, Gabriela." In Linda's voice, Gaby almost thought she heard wistful echoes of friendship, however long ago it had existed. How altered they were now.

An uncertain smile was the only answer she could give as she departed.

ELI PACED, AS HE HAD EVER since he'd detoured by her house when he should have been resting. Instead, he'd lain awake, imagining Gaby with Chad.

It shouldn't matter. He had no business being here. She had no place in his quest.

She needed to return to New York, where she'd be safe from the coil of scandal and murder he was attempting to unwind without the benefit of help from the experts. He was alone in this journey to clear himself.

If she'd simply go, he'd never have to talk to her again. There was nothing to discuss, anyway. He'd been hurt, but he was over her. They'd been kids, and he'd gotten too involved. Believed they'd shared more than they had.

Yet despite all that, he wanted to see her again.

But only to ask her why she'd walked away so easily. Left him behind like a summer fling.

Fool. Idiot.

Paco shied from the ferocity of his brush strokes. Dirt rose in puffs from the horse's coat.

"Sorry, pal. The woman's got me all worked up." He forced himself to slow the pace. To relax tense muscles. It was nothing to him what Gaby did with her time. If she had an itch to spend every day and night with that slick son of a—

Eli whirled and threw the brush as hard as

he could into the pen outside the barn. It sailed over the fence and out of sight.

Paco shifted, and Eli fought to get a grip on himself. To be here in daylight was foolish. He couldn't chance revealing the location of his hideout. He had nowhere else to stay that wouldn't expose others to the risk of attracting Chad Anderson's attention.

He released a long, frustrated sigh and let his head fall back against the side of the stall. To contemplate waiting hours in the confines of his cave with only mental images of Chad's hands on her, his—

The sound of an engine roused him. He crossed to the door.

Gaby. Time for him to slip away. He watched for his chance as she carried groceries inside.

But she reemerged too quickly. Started toward the barn.

The dog darted toward her like a bullet.

She smiled, and it was like basking in sunshine. "Hey, Buddy!" She knelt and indulged in a good rub. After a couple of minutes of petting, she sank her face into the dog's neck and simply held on. "Thanks, fella. Just what the doctor ordered."

Eli observed from the shadows.

And envied the dog.

But when Gaby rose and approached the barn, he was forced into action. The structure was simple and small, with few places to hide. If he'd had a little more warning, he could have caught a rafter and swung into position over her head.

If he hadn't spent precious seconds gazing at her.

But too late for that. He ducked into the shadowy recesses of the stall across and one down from Paco's. If he angled his body just right, he could still spot the horse.

And still view the girl who had haunted his dreams. How beautiful she was. Definitely a woman now, and ripe for a man's hands.

Damn it. *She's not for you. She never was.*

And she'd abandoned him when he'd needed her most.

"Hey, boy," she crooned as she approached Paco. The horse eagerly stuck his head over the bars. "I don't have a treat for you. I'm sorry."

Here, where she assumed herself unobserved except by animals, she sounded more like the eager girl who'd shared herself so freely with him, her unfettered thoughts, her most ambitious hopes...her fears and her dreams.

Oh, those had been the days. Man, they'd been young—or she had, at least. He wasn't certain he'd ever been a kid. Nonetheless, for the priceless hours they were able to steal, he'd been less wary than usual, more willing to venture into trust.

Big mistake.

She extended one slender hand over Paco's muzzle, giggling faintly as the horse sucked her fingers into his mouth. "Oh, you sweet baby...what am I going to do with you when I go?" She laid the side of her head against his and stroked over his jaw.

When I go. She would, of course.

She shook her hair back and straightened. He saw the glimmer of tears on her cheeks and hardened his heart to remember what was at stake.

"Surely Papa has some kind of treat out here." She stopped. Bit her lip. "Had, I mean." For a second, her expression was devastated, then once again she gathered herself.

Grudgingly, Eli admired her control. The vulnerable girl he'd loved had fulfilled the promise of strength he'd predicted.

Then she turned in his direction.

Eli pressed himself into the darkest corner, suddenly and surprisingly not ready. For years, he'd longed to have it out with her, to learn why she'd let him down. Make her admit she'd lied. That she'd never really loved him after all.

Now he wasn't sure what he wanted.

Gaby drew nearly even with his position, and he absorbed every detail: the tiny mole just below her right ear, the sleek sable of her hair, the lovely curve of her lips.

Her step faltered, almost as if she sensed his presence. Her head swiveled in his direction.

Eli held himself motionless.

Then the dog trotted right through the opening of the stall.

Headed directly for him.

"WHAT IS IT, BOY?" Gaby asked. "What do you—"

Movement, there in the shadows. Her throat clenched. *This isn't the city,* Chad had warned. She began to back away, seeking something to use as a weapon. "Here, Buddy. Get back. You'll—"

A man stepped out of the shadows. Big. Strong. Unsmiling.

She tensed. Prepared to flee. "Who are you? What do you—"

Then blue eyes locked on hers. A huge fist closed around her breastbone. Shoved out all room for breath.

Eli. So changed he was.

But deep in her blood, in her marrow, she knew him.

He stared at her without speaking, and she devoured him with her own gaze, cataloging the differences. The years had transformed nearly everything about him—he was taller, more muscled, his dark hair was longer, the bones of his face had emerged.

But those solemn eyes that had once been her world...

"Eli." A whisper was all she could manage. She summoned muscles gone slack with shock and moved forward, wishing—

What? To rewind the clock? To undo all their mistakes? If such could be managed, she'd alter so many things, all the way back to when he'd been beaten and left for dead in the desert.

Except then, all those other nights wouldn't have existed, nor would the golden moments they'd had together in darkness. Food for her soul, however devastating their end was.

She swallowed to moisten a throat gone desert dry. "Why are you here?" The words were harsher than she'd intended.

One dark eyebrow rose. "Good question." His voice was cold, distant. Nothing like the one she'd heard in her sleep. Or that of the boy she'd loved.

"Chad is hunting you," she managed to say at last. "For killing my father."

"Maybe you should call him," he challenged.

She blinked. "But—"

"Leave, Gaby. Go home to New York."

Betrayal was a poison-filled dart. "You— you knew where I was all this time, and you didn't—" *Come to me?*

"That was over long ago."

If ever she'd dreamed—and she had—of a future meeting, she'd pictured them falling into each other's arms, that the magic would be there again, only stronger. They'd make love, and it would be unforgettable. Life altering.

She tore herself from memory to reality. The stern man who stood before her was no one she'd ever met.

The chasm between them hurt more than it should have. She reached for her pride. "No, we've outgrown childish folly." She wondered if anything she'd believed back then had been true. "I'm going to New York as soon as possible." Only this second had she decided that. Forget the two weeks. "There's nothing for me here."

He studied her with a look that seemed to go straight through her. "So simple to walk away from the people who need you."

Her eyes widened. *You cheered me on. Told me to aim high. And you left me first.* "I have another life now. I'm moving up in the world."

"The world's a big place," he mocked. "I find that New York has an inflated sense of its own importance. Not everything's about money or fame."

Never, not once, had he been cruel to her. Made fun of her. "I've worked hard to get where I am."

"And where is that, Gaby? A magazine

focused on the insecurities of women? Slaves to fashion or the latest fad diet?"

Despite her own recent misgivings, she resented his dismissal of everything she'd accomplished, even as she raged at his obvious familiarity with details of her existence. The realization that he could have contacted her before now. "Who are you to tell me what's worthwhile? You have no right, not after you—"

"Quiet—"

She bristled—then she heard a vehicle's roar up the road leading to this house.

He grasped her arm and yanked her into the shadows with him.

Memories swamped her at the touch of his hand. "Let go of me."

"It's lover boy." He released her abruptly. "Go on. Tell him I'm here." His eyes blistered hers with challenge.

But she recalled how he'd always used bravado to mask fear. "However much you've changed, I won't believe you had anything to do with my father's death."

A second of what might be gratitude flickered, instantly shuttered. "Oh, I was definitely involved, but I didn't kill him."

"What do you mean—"

Just then, Chad's pickup braked to a halt.

"Stay here," she said. "We need to talk."

"There's nothing to discuss."

She paused at the entrance to the stall to cast him one astonished glance. "You can't possibly be serious."

Chad's door slammed. Angry strides took him to the front door. When no one answered, he dropped from the porch and stalked around. "Gabriela—" he shouted.

"I'm going to send him on his way, then I'll be back."

"Don't. Stay out of this."

"It's my father who died." She dug in. "Promise you'll return to me after dark, when it's safer."

"No. Pack up and get out."

"I won't. I'll come looking for you. Eli, I'm even more stubborn than before."

She thought his lips curved slightly, but all too soon, his features snapped back to grim resolve. "You won't find me." With one decisive push, he forced her into the light.

GABY STRUGGLED TO SHOVE Eli from her mind. Render her face impassive.

"Hi, Chad." Her heart was pounding so loudly she was dizzy. "Are you okay?" As quickly as possible, she put distance between herself and the barn.

"I called, and you didn't answer." He shrugged. "I got worried."

"I went into town to buy groceries. I'm a big girl, Chad."

"You are." His expression was unrepentant. "Mostly I wanted an excuse to see you."

"We had breakfast." Her nerves screamed with the knowledge that Eli was only yards away.

Even if he cared not one whit about having her protection, it appeared.

But she had unanswered questions.

"Gabriela?"

"What? Sorry." She summoned a smile. "I guess I'm a little weary."

"I asked if you'd let me take you to dinner tonight."

She had other plans, not that she could tell Chad.

What if she was wrong, and Eli had killed her father?

No. He was different, harder, but she could not believe that of him.

Oh, I was definitely involved, but I didn't kill him.

She couldn't afford for Chad to become suspicious.

Placing one hand on his arm, she smiled up at him. "A rain check, maybe? I'm so tired I wouldn't be good company. I'm going to make an early night of it."

"All right." He lifted one hand to her hair. "You're worth waiting for."

"Thank you, Chad." Part of her squirmed with guilt for her subterfuge, but she still felt a strong urge to shield Eli, however little the grown man resembled the boy.

To soothe her conscience at the lie, she rose to her toes and kissed Chad's cheek.

His expression spoke of wanting more from her, and he bent closer.

Keenly aware of Eli's presence in the barn, she hastily retreated. "Thank you for worrying about me. I swear I'll be fine."

"Waiting doesn't come real naturally to me, Gabriela."

She smiled but didn't speak.

Chad touched the brim of his hat. "I'll phone you." Then he got into his truck and drove off.

Gaby was careful to remain in place until he was out of sight.

Then she pivoted and returned the way she'd come.

"Eli," she called out as she entered the barn. "If you don't show up, I'll be out there searching for you."

She heard no answer. Searched the entire structure.

Already certain Eli would be gone.

DAMN IT, DAMN IT, DAMN IT.

But it was he who was damned—by the force of longing he didn't welcome. Watching her with Chad, witnessing her touching him, recognizing the hunger in Chad because he had his own.

He had an itch to pound the bastard.

Instead, he circled behind the barn, then past the rear of Gaby's truck and slipped into the morning shade cast by the far side of her house. The high desert afforded few obvious hiding places until you arrived at the foothills of the Davis Mountains, but even desert landscapes were not perfectly flat. The land, however sere and barren to city eyes, still possessed secrets for a man with patience.

If only he felt patient right now. He shook his entire body as if to cast away his craving for her the way a dog sheds water.

Years' worth of hurt had made him rough with her, yet she'd stood up to him. His insides were a tangle of anger and lost hope, of longing to forget everything but him and her.

One simple touch had shattered his defenses. Pierced the lid over his emotions, a seal he'd convinced himself was steel strong, only to discover that it could be rent like tissue paper.

The Eli I knew had a gentle heart.

The bond between him and Gaby had been almost supernatural, but she had been only a girl, naive and virginal, however valiant.

The Gaby he'd met today was not the same person. She'd found her world, the one he'd always understood he'd lose her to. She'd prospered without him.

Which was fine. Good.

But it still hurt. And the notion of her with Chad enraged him.

I'm even more stubborn than before. I'll come looking for you.

Eli reached the mouth of his cave and didn't stifle a rueful smile. She'd do it, too. He had to stop her. Convince her to go.

He couldn't allow her to venture into the seamy tangle he was struggling to unravel to prove his innocence. She might think she was tough, but there were forces at work she couldn't imagine. The responsibility was his to uncover a means—and quickly so—to send her racing back to the life she had sought.

Away from him…and the danger he had always posed to her.

He shook his hand and tried again to erase the feel of her from a mind that craved only to cradle her close.

CHAPTER SEVEN

SHE WAS EXHAUSTED and confused. Hurt and angry. She yearned to lie down and give up. Return to New York and stop all this anguish.

But giving up wasn't in her, so, too agitated to wait around and skeptical that Eli would do as she'd asked, Gaby took action. She drove down a dusty, one-lane road, keeping herself alert for the mailbox belonging to a reclusive old woman, Juanita Alvarez, a friend of Eli's mother. She was reputed to be a *bruja*, a witch. Gaby had asked Eli about her once, but he'd cut short any sort of discussion.

Would the old woman have an idea where Eli was staying? Was she in touch with him? Or was she even still alive?

The mailbox had always been a source of interest, both outraged and amused, in

Chamizal. Señora Alvarez was seldom in town, but her mailbox often sported displays that people said bore curses or spells, odd concoctions of flowers and bird feathers, of dried seed pods and unnamed plant stems, often woven with bits of colorful ribbons. Some remained there for weeks or even months, but others were replaced in a matter of days. A young Gaby had once attempted to decipher them with books she'd checked out from the bookmobile.

Other than refining Gaby's recognition of plants and flowers, however, the search had done little to answer her questions.

As she neared the mailbox, she noted that the display appeared fresh, the purple ribbon bright and the marigold petals plump as if just picked.

She turned down the road that led to the *bruja*'s house, reminding herself that she was an educated woman currently living in one of the most sophisticated cities in the world. *Brujas* were a superstition out of her culture's past and had no place in the present, however sinister their connotation.

A half mile or so down this dusty excuse for a road lay a small adobe cottage. Gaby

had, like most local children, crept down
this path at night on a dare, scalp prickling
with equal parts thrill and terror. It was a rite
of passage to risk touching the witch's
mailbox display, then make the walk under
the light of a full moon, trembling each step,
to place a flower as close as possible to the
old woman's front door.

Gaby had decried the practice to Linda
and two other friends, dismissing it as pure
nonsense, but in the end, she'd gone along
and even led the procession.

The others had chickened out at the
bruja's front gate, but Gaby had tiptoed all
the way to the front porch, her heart
thumping nearly out of her chest, to lay her
own offering, one of her mother's roses.

She'd thought she'd seen a twitch of the
front curtains, and at the last minute, she'd
been terrified that the witch would curse her
family. Gaby had snatched the rose back and
run all the way home, enduring the jeering of
her companions without ever explaining her
actions.

A few months later, Gaby's mother had
died. Consumed by shock and grief, Gaby
had not remembered the escapade at first.

But in the inescapable chain of questioning—*what could I have done to prevent this?*—that accompanies a loss, that night had popped into Gaby's mind and refused to budge. Too scared and consumed by guilt, she never told anyone about her premonition and, she recognized now, only cemented more in her own mind that she had played a part in killing her mother.

A child's superstition, the adult Gaby understood, one banished by the light of reason. But for an instant, she stared through the windshield at the weathered structure and could feel the earth beneath her smaller feet, could smell the mingled scents of the old woman's garden and her own mother's rose, could hear her heartbeat unnaturally loud in the menacing darkness as she ran and ran and ran—

Then the front door of the little house opened, and Gaby snapped back into the present.

Two women emerged, one smaller than the other, both bearing the marks of time's passage in their frames. They stood and simply observed her as though waiting with endless patience, what she could view of their faces from here, only mildly curious and kind.

Somehow, driving forward seemed presumptuous, rude even, so she shut off the engine and emerged from the cab of the old pickup. She began to walk toward them, reminding the child inside her that *brujas* were like unicorns, a flight of fancy only. She searched in her mind for a proper greeting, a way to begin the conversation, but the stillness of the two women seemed to drain every last thought from her head.

She halted before them and studied them as they were regarding her. Both were Latinas, one taller than Gaby and one so diminutive she appeared almost elfin. Gaby was not tall herself, a matter of chagrin since she had discovered in New York that people treat small women differently, attributing childlike status to them.

The tall woman was fierce; the tiny woman radiated peace so vividly that Gaby's defenses weakened.

She was so exhausted. So confused, about Eli and Chad and her father. About her life in New York and the visceral pull of this place, the memories around every corner—

She found herself longing to sink to her knees and rest her head against the tiny woman's skirts.

The small woman smiled and extended a hand. "Come, child. Have tea with us."

Gaby was startled. "Tea?" She darted a glance at the taller woman. A witch's tea? Inevitable comparisons to Alice dining with the Red Queen raced through her head.

The small woman laughed. "Stop glowering, Juanita. You're frightening the child."

"You're Frank's daughter," the tall woman, who must be Juanita Alvarez, said. Her tone wasn't welcoming.

"Yes." Gaby refused to back down, however much accusation was in the woman's voice.

The tiny woman clasped Gaby's hand, and Gaby was suffused with a calm that overrode everything else. "I am Adelaida Montalvo, Juanita's friend. I am visiting from La Paloma."

La Paloma was another village nearer to Alpine. "I'm Gaby—Gabriela Navarro," she said. "And I'm interrupting. I'll just go now."

But Adelaida did not release her hand. "You must have tea with us first," she insisted. "I am sorry for your loss. Your father was a good man."

"You knew him?" Gaby was as surprised by that statement as by her illogical reaction to this woman.

"I did. He and Juanita were close friends."

"He and—" Gaby's gaze was immediately drawn to the unsmiling woman as she struggled to absorb the notion that both her father and Eli had been connected to Juanita Alvarez. "How long did you know him?" she asked the taller woman.

"He visited me after your mother died."

"Why?"

"Why would you care? You left him."

"Juanita," Señora Montalvo cautioned. "Grasp her hand. Feel for yourself the depth of her grief. She loves him."

Gaby clenched her free hand at her waist and snatched the other one from Señora Montalvo's grip, as well. "What do you mean, feel for yourself?" She glanced at Señora Alvarez. "*Brujas* are a superstition of the ignorant."

The two women exchanged looks. Then Señora Montalvo sighed. "She is not a *bruja,* though she enjoys the freedom that reputation grants her." Mischief sparked in the smaller woman's eyes. "I would not advise you to be so quick to dismiss centuries of tradition. The Anglo world puts you at war with your heritage, does it not?" She shook her head. "I understand. My grandsons have fought this battle. Diego has made his peace and found a way to incorporate his Western medical training with his destiny as a *curandero*. Jesse's struggle between his former career in law enforcement and his immense talent as an artist has not been so easy."

"A *curandero?*" Gaby stifled the urge to roll her eyes. "That's another superstition. There are quacks everywhere cashing in on the public interest in herbal medicine."

"Oh, child." Señora Montalvo clucked her tongue. "You have strayed so far from your culture. Do you think me fearsome or crooked?"

Gaby's eyes widened. "You're a *curandera?*"

"All my life," the woman said. "As is Juanita. It is a long and honorable tradition."

Gaby's mouth dropped open. "You?" she said to the taller woman. Her mind flew back to the bouquets her mother had placed all over the house after yet another miscarriage. *Do not disturb them,* mijita. *They are prayers for the baby's soul. Offerings, that the next one will stay with us in this world.*

Little altars her mother had tucked into this corner and that. No *Día de los Muertos* celebrations for babies who never breathed, but her mother had created her own memorials.

But no parties. No *mole.* No marigolds.

"The small bouquets in our house each time she lost a baby." Gaby stared at Juanita Alvarez. "That was you?"

"*Sí.*"

"She always believed that the next baby would stay." A lump crowded Gaby's throat. "You told her that. You took advantage—"

Señora Montalvo laid one gentle hand on her arm. "Easy, *mija.* Did the herbs help?"

Gaby shook her off. "She cried. Over and over. She assumed I didn't see. My father desired a son, and she was determined to provide him with one because I—" *Wasn't enough. Was only a girl.* "You killed her," Gaby said through gritted teeth, understanding even then how absurd the charge was. Fast in the grip of bitterness and loss she'd thought she was over, she wanted someone else to hurt as much as she was. "You kept her hope alive, and she continued to try for the son my father craved, until she was too weak to fight off a simple flu. You helped that happen—"

Black dots danced. White sparks showered, obscured her vision. Gaby bent double, clutching her middle, and a sliver of the howl that had been lacerating her insides for days slipped through her lips. The air swirled around her, and an awful wind rushed through her head, a sirocco that screamed until she was deaf—

Hands held her, soothed her. Buttressed her as the floor rushed to meet her—

But Gaby was lost in old grief and new grief and the endless pain she'd pushed down and down and down—

Until she'd had enough. And grief consumed all that she was.

SHE CAME TO ON A SMALL bed. In a room both spare and beautiful.

Incense, rich and sweet, curled in the air around her. A murmur twined with it, a dance that soothed. Succored. Past her feet, the warm glow of candles cast out the shadows of oncoming night.

Gaby girded herself to rise.

A fingertip, only one, pressed to the space between her eyebrows. Warmth flowed deep inside her.

"Your heart is weary, child. Breathe, only breathe, for now. Grant your heart rest." The strong voice. The taller woman who had—

Hurt Mama. But in that moment, Gaby couldn't summon the will to resist. She ached, clear to her bones. She craved more of the peace that streamed into her at the touch of this woman's hands.

As if she'd spoken, the finger tapped between her brows three times. Chants as solemn as prayers spilled over her, covering her with an invisible cloak, sealing in warmth, shoving back the cold that had claimed squatter's rights in her chest.

"Tired," she whispered, though she wasn't sure her lips had moved. Her eyelids could not.

"Rest. Let go," said the other voice, the soft one that made her long to lie down for a hundred years.

The air over her body stirred. On the

wings of a faint breeze, she smelled something...

Romero. Rosemary. Drifting, perfuming... sweeping in arcs down the length of her, outward from shoulder to shoulder in the shape of a cross, accompanied, ever and always, by first one voice, then two, a melody of comfort, a symphony of ease. Gaby had a fleeting thought to resist...in a minute...in a little...

"Nothing can harm you here, *niña,*" said the soft voice.

"You are safe," intoned the stronger one.

The small, frightened creature inside Gaby released a slow breath...curled up—

And, for the first time in longer than she could remember, sank into a place of peace.

And slept. Sweetly, simply...slept.

WHEN GABY AWOKE AGAIN, dawn was pearling the sky, that faint lightening of darkest navy hovering at the edge of the horizon. She shifted, feeling—

She frowned, not certain exactly what she did feel. Slightly sore, in a pleasant manner, the way you do after a good massage worked out muscles that have been cramped and strained for too long.

Lighter, as well, though she was equally unable to put a finger on exactly what had changed.

She stretched, and a delicious shiver went through her. She felt…stronger; that was it. Refreshed after the best slumber she could recall in…ever.

She smiled and opened her eyes.

Then sat up fast.

This was not her apartment. Not her room at… home.

The space, barely larger than a monk's cell, was a place she'd never been. White-washed walls relieved only by an altar across from the single bed on which she'd slept. A cross, of course, but not a crucifix. Two figures, the Virgin Mary and the Virgin of Guadalupe. Candles, many of them, in blue and red and only one white.

And stems of rosemary.

Gaby blinked. Noted the light outside. *Oh, no. Morning.* If Eli had returned last night as she'd asked—

She shoved from the bed and nearly tripped on the hem of her—

Nightgown?

"Buenas días."

Her head whipped in the direction of the door. Juanita Alvarez stood there with a solemn expression.

But kind eyes.

Gaby frowned. Stared past her.

"Adelaida is brewing tea."

Gaby plucked at the white cotton that covered her. She had the notion that she should be angry.

But she felt too good. Still—

"What did you do to me?" she demanded.

Juanita sighed and shook her head. Held out a hand. "I told Adelaida I was the wrong one to approach you first. Come with me."

Odd fragments floated up then, little bubbles rising to the surface and popping open.

Rosemary. Soft air currents. Incense.

Comfort.

Gaby wavered, shifting bare feet over the smooth wood floors.

Juanita's hand remained outstretched, her eyes both chiding and patient, as if there was all the time in the world for Gaby to make up her mind.

You are safe.

In this woman was strength in abundance.

Gaby's own seemed to have fled. "Tell me what happened here." More a plea than a demand.

Juanita nodded. "Over tea." She opened the door wider.

"I start my day with coffee."

"Too often, I am certain. This day, you will not." She turned and walked out as if certain Gaby would follow.

To her own surprise, Gaby did just that.

SUSTO. GABY ROLLED the word around in her head, but it was her heart that heard the diagnosis.

"Your soul has been driven from your body by the shock of your father's passing," said Juanita. "You would grow weaker if we did not rid you of the darkness preventing its return."

"What was all that—" Gaby waved toward the little room. "Last night? The… chanting. The candles. The rosemary."

"You are a child of your culture, however much you have become estranged," chided Adelaida. "You know of *curanderismo.*"

Yes, of course, she did. Many people swore by the native healers who kept alive traditions extending all the way back to the Aztecs and enriched by assimilating the wisdom the Moors had brought to Spain, the practices of the Africans who had arrived as slaves in the Caribbean. Core beliefs of Catholicism had mingled, as well, and the stew was a potent one.

Curanderas were the doctor of choice for many. Medical care was sparse in this region and, as everywhere, too expensive for all but the wealthy or the insured. Health coverage was nonexistent for a huge segment of the population across the country, and alternative medicine was a growing interest through all socioeconomic levels.

But not for Gaby. As an adult, she was a Harvard-med-school-grad kind of patient, the exceedingly rare times she'd sought out a doctor. As a kid, she'd hardly ever been sick, and county health-department clinics had taken care of her vaccinations. Her father had scoffed at what he'd called witch doctors.

Her mother, apparently, had not.

"I...don't know what to think." Gaby clutched the pottery cup of tea.

The two women traded smiling glances. "You should meet my Diego and his Caroline. My grandson is half Latino and trained in Western medicine, but he is heir to my abilities. He was torn between two worlds for a long time, and when he met Caroline, she was a famous cardiac surgeon who only tolerated my practices because she loved me."

"What happened to them?"

Adelaida's smile was fond and proud. "They went through many hard times before they found a place of peace. Now they operate clinics both in La Paloma and Dallas, where Caroline practiced, and they incorporate the best of both worlds for the benefit of those who would otherwise have no medical care. Diego tends my patients now, along with many others, and thus I am free to visit my friend, a luxury I did not have for many years."

"A busman's holiday?" Gaby asked with a smile. Cleansed by the storm of tears, if not reassured by the explanations she'd received from the two old women, Gaby nonetheless had to admit that she was feeling better than she had in a long time.

Probably only the sound night's sleep.

Adelaida nodded patiently. "A healer can never turn away from those in need." Her expression grew solemn. "I am leaving today. Diego will fetch me soon. If you will excuse me, I must pack." At the door, she paused. "You must allow Juanita to help you. You are not out of danger." With measured steps, she proceeded down the hall.

Gaby looked at the other woman. "I have to return to New York as soon as I can dispose of my father's place."

"It would kill Frank all over again to hear you speak in that manner," Juanita said.

The wisps of peace fled. "I have no choice. I can't live here. My life's in Manhattan."

Juanita's head shook slowly. "You will have no life until you come to terms with your past. With your father." She paused. "With Eli."

Eli. "Have you seen him? I have to find him. Chad is hunting for him. He's convinced Eli killed my father."

Nothing showed on Juanita's face, but her eyes were an eagle's. "And what do you believe?"

"He left me." In that instant, she realized just how deep the hurt still went. "Without a word. Maybe I never really knew him."

If anything, Juanita's face hardened. "Perhaps you did not." Her tone indicted Gaby, however, not Eli.

"I worried about him." Gaby was surprised to hear herself admit it. "I searched for him everywhere, but after the fire killed his mother, he vanished."

Silence was the only response, but she was certain that this woman was her best chance to find him. "He would not hurt his mother—I don't care what anyone claims," Gaby said.

No answer but preternatural stillness, as if Gaby still had something to prove.

"He wouldn't have harmed my father—at least, the boy I loved wouldn't have." The word *love* echoed all around her, one she hadn't dared voice for a long time. That emotion wasn't on her radar screen and hadn't been for years.

Nine, to be exact. She wasn't sure what would be required to make her risk her heart again.

Juanita rose then but paused, aging hands

on the scarred wooden surface of the table. Lovely hands, Gaby noticed, for all that time had marked them. Comforting and strong.

"Your Sheriff Anderson thinks otherwise."

"I know. He's determined to find Eli and put him away. If he's still nearby, Eli should leave." She laid her own hand atop the old woman's, and something passed between them, a current strong enough to reach into Gaby's heart. "Please…make him go. Tell him—"

What to say to a man who bore no resemblance to the boy who had once been her world? She was changed, as well, perhaps too much.

But for the boy's sake, she took a chance. "Tell him that I—I don't want harm to come to him, whatever has changed between us."

Juanita's eyes darkened then. "Tell him yourself. Eli will not visit me now, to protect me from that man's son." Her tone held a bitter note.

"What man? Do you mean Chad's father? What does he have to do with this? And why do you need protecting?"

"Adelaida," Juanita called out. "I must

show you one more thing before you go." Juanita picked up her mug and left the table with slow steps.

Gaby stood. "Wait—" She grasped at Juanita's arm, but the old woman stiffened. "At least give me something to help me locate him."

Juanita relented only slightly. "Your heart could do that." She shook her head. "But only if you are willing to listen." With immense dignity, she departed.

Gaby stared after her for endless moments.

Then finally, she shook her head and made her way to the small room to dress.

CHAPTER EIGHT

WHERE THE DEVIL WAS SHE? Eli paced in the shadows of the barn. Against his better judgment, he'd returned after sunset, only to discover her gone. When he should have been out patrolling, instead he'd made three trips back here during the night.

But Gaby had never made it home.

He pondered what he'd witnessed—Gaby on tiptoes, kissing Chad's cheek. Chad's obvious desire for her.

His gut twisted at the notion of the two of them together, the man who was determined to destroy him and the faithless woman—

However much you've changed, I won't believe you had anything to do with my father's death.

She wasn't faithless, then. But why, when she'd been so insistent that he return to her, had she been gone all night?

The only answers were ones he couldn't tolerate. She was with Chad.

Or, worse, Chad's partners had made a move on her.

And Eli had no one to ask. Nowhere to seek help.

Mingled fear and fury tore at him until he thought he—

The sound of an engine. An old one.

Eli peered from the barn and spotted Gaby driving up. Nearly went to his knees in relief.

Until he spotted Chad's truck right behind her.

CHAD'S EXPRESSION was grim as he rounded the hood of his truck. "Where have you been?"

All traces of his previous charm were gone. "Why is it any of your business?"

His face darkened, but he gathered himself in, though a muscle in his tight jaw leaped. "You never came home last night."

"So?"

"Until we have Wolverton in custody, you're not safe."

"Eli would never hurt me."

His gaze on her was pure steel. "You're a fool if you believe that."

"And here I was sure I was a grown woman who'd been on her own for a long time. I can take care of myself just fine, thank you."

The strong jaw tightened. "You're out of your league now."

She couldn't help the laughter that burst from her. "No, I'm not. Chad, do you have any idea what it's like to be a woman alone in New York at night? Do you have a clue how many locks I have on my apartment door?"

He stiffened with damaged pride. "I'm only trying to keep you from harm."

Patience, Gaby. You're in macho country. "I appreciate your concern, but I'm not your responsibility."

He focused tawny eyes on her. "You could be," he said softly.

"Chad..." She was treading dangerous ground now. She chose to dodge. "My father just died. I don't know what I want right now." That much was God's honest truth.

His shoulders eased a little. "I under-stand." He backed away, holding the door open for her. "I'm doing everything I can to bring his murderer to justice."

She descended and stood in front of him, forcibly restraining herself from arguing over Eli's innocence. "I know you are."

"Until I have him in custody, you could be a target." His stance was stubborn. "You should stay with me. If you need a damn chaperone, María is there to guard your virtue," he grumbled.

Gaby couldn't stem a chuckle. "Chad, my virtue hightailed it years ago."

It was the wrong thing to say, bringing to mind how often Chad had attempted to sweet talk her into surrendering her virginity to him. How she'd cooled toward him once Eli had come into her life.

She drew back from him, and the sudden silence between them echoed with old hurts. "I promise to be careful, but that's all you can ask of me. I've been on my own too long to be tucked under anyone's wing now. Anyway, I'll be gone soon."

His glance sharpened. "Will you? Have you given any more consideration to what you'd like to do with the ranch? I'll buy it from you, if that's what you wish. Make you a good price for it, too. You can clear out whatever you feel like, then I can either dispose of the rest or put it in storage until you're ready to handle it." Here he paused, his gaze locked on hers. "But what I'd prefer to do is what our fathers had planned."

She wasn't ready, not for a proposal or, she was surprised to discover, for the notion of quickly divesting herself of the ranch. "When I figure that out, you'll be the first to know. That's all I can promise right now."

A mulish expression on his face, he nodded. "I should be getting to the office," he said stiffly.

"Have a good day," she offered.

He tipped the brim of his hat, then got into his truck. He left a cloud of dust behind him as he shot down the drive.

Gaby shook her head and sighed. Men. One who was invisible, and one who wouldn't leave her alone.

Had Eli returned last night? If not, she was going after him. Juanita was right—Gaby did understand some things about him. First she'd check the cave where he'd often holed up.

And with that resolution, something inside

her settled for the first time since she'd picked up the phone in New York. She would dig into all that she'd been avoiding, however painful, and figure out what had been happening just before her father's death. She had learned much about financial matters under her boss's tutelage, and she would use all that in a quest to uncover who might benefit from her father's demise. Who would benefit by having him out of the way—and why.

Chad, as a neighbor, would welcome the opportunity to own this land, of course, but there must be others with interests more sinister than simply being next door.

At last, she had a purpose. Something more concrete than grief, something that would allow her to utilize her brain instead of permit her to wallow in all the emotions she'd been dredging up for days now.

Her boss had told her often that no one could divine the heart of the matter more quickly or swing into action more decisively.

She walked inside the house, mentally rolling up her sleeves.

Work had been her salvation for a long time. It would be so again.

PAWING THROUGH THE SMALL wooden desk felt like trespassing, but she had no choice. Her father was not here to ask. Tucked into a corner of the living room, the desk had been off-limits to her for so much of her life that she found herself touching the center drawer pull, then yanking her hand back as though a spanking awaited.

She couldn't help a small shake of her head at how deeply ingrained childhood prohibitions could become. She opened the drawer and stared at the contents.

A date book from 1997, one given out by the feed store in Alpine. It was stuffed with bits of paper and held closed by a worn rubber band.

Three stubby pencils and two ballpoint pens, one bearing the logo of her father's bank, long since absorbed into one of the endless chains of superbanks spreading across the country.

A handful of rusty paper clips.

Several sheets of notebook paper like that she'd used in school.

One small folded sheet, creased with age. Gingerly, she picked it up and opened it.

Her own handwriting greeted her, if a younger version:

Papi—
I am spending the night with Linda.
You and Paco behave!
Te amo.
Gabriela

The sheer artlessness of the note, the easy assumption that he wouldn't be lonely, that she was entitled to fly free and never think about whether he would miss her or appreciate her cooking his supper because he was exhausted—

Te amo. I love you. Her eyes filmed over.

I did love you, Papa. I still do. I am so very sorry for all the years we lost, for all the talks we could have had when I was more mature. When I could have understood that you were not simply mi padre, *the authority figure in my life, but you were a man trying to do his best to raise a motherless daughter when you were drowning in grief yourself.*

She ached for the man who'd helped her make the transition into womanhood, who'd negotiated the terrifying swamp of teenage-girl fashion and dating etiquette. Who had attended as many school programs as possible, sometimes arriving late and dust covered but still there in the back of the room, hat in hand, eyes intent on her performance or speech or song.

Oh, God. What did I do to you, Papa, when I left? When my hurt and my pride refused us a chance?

The pain of picturing him, here in this house, alone and deprived of a future, nearly drove her to her knees. She was his child, his heir. She should be focusing on justice and not waiting for Chad Anderson. Eli could not have killed him—believing otherwise was more than she could bear—but what had gone on between them?

Why, after all these years, was Eli here?

Questions circled her like vultures, each ready to seize her at the first sign of surrender. She set the note aside and picked up the date book, slipping off the rubber band—

But it snapped, too brittle to withstand yet another pull.

I won't be like that. Whatever I find out, I can handle.

She settled into the creaking desk chair

and began to turn the pages. Most of the notations had to do with animals and crops. She determined early on that they had no relationship to the dates in this book but were, more likely, simply a result of her father's unwillingness to let anything go to waste. Here was paper; he would use it.

Records of animal-feed purchases and inoculations, of seeds sown and times of harvest, along with yields. The stray bits of paper were an assortment of receipts and reminders to himself, each written in the crabbed hand he used to maximize how much information he could record on a single page.

She flipped another sheet, and a tiny envelope fell into her lap. Gently, she set the book aside and turned the envelope over, hesitating when she noticed that it was sealed. She felt the contents and realized there was a key inside. She chewed on her lip and reminded herself that all this belonged to her now. She pressed the brown paper between her fingers, then carefully unfastened the flap and emptied the contents into her hand.

A key indeed, with no inscription on it, but it looked like—

A safe-deposit box key?

Papa didn't own anything valuable enough to require that security, or he hadn't, all those years ago. He'd cherished her mother's wedding ring and a lock of her hair, but he'd kept those with him—

Gaby stifled a sob. Those things had never left his body, encased in a small bag like a Native American totem, worn around his neck. Her parents had been too poor to afford a wedding band for him, but he would not have parted with the one he'd bought for her mother.

The lock of hair would be ashes. A shudder rippled through her as her mind shied away from the horrifying image she'd been working very hard not to think about ever since she'd rounded the corner of the house the first day with Chad.

But the simple gold ring, delicate as it was, would not have burned, would it? Was it still there, in the rubble of the barn in which her father had died? She nearly rose from the chair to search for it, but everything she'd been holding at bay swamped her, grisly images she hadn't wanted to imagine. Couldn't bear to, or she'd go mad.

Then she noted the afternoon shadows lengthening and understood that she was in for a rough night if she didn't face what lay out there waiting.

Chad would likely possess the answer, but today's encounter still rankled. Chad might believe Eli was in the area, but that was a long way from proving it. If Eli was still as good at hiding himself as he'd once been, Chad would be forced to examine every inch of ground for many square miles to have hope of finding him.

Chad didn't know, as Gaby did, Eli's former hideouts. He might not still be in any of them, but now that she was certain he hadn't left Chamizal, she had a place to start.

First, however, she had to make herself confront the place where her father had died. She was not a coward, and she dishonored her father by her fear. If she was to help Eli prove he was not her father's killer, she would need every ounce of courage she'd spent years alone developing.

HE HAD WORK TO DO, damn it. She was in no position to make an ultimatum. There wasn't time for him to go to her again tonight.

But he had to see her. That simple.

A wry half grin curved his mouth. There was nothing simple about his Gaby, never had been.

Not his Gaby anymore, though. No matter how his body tightened at the mere thought of her, now that he'd caught the scent of her. Pressed his skin against hers.

Oh, hell, why didn't he just admit he was going, no matter how illogical it was? He was more than halfway there already.

Eli went to alert suddenly. Motion in the distance. He grabbed the binoculars from his pack.

Then relaxed as the nameless dog raced toward him. Poor guy, torn between his rescuer and a woman Eli would like to curl up with himself. Yearned to have his hands all over—

He swore and yanked his mind away from something that wasn't going to happen, a dream even a naive boy with only a basic understanding of the mechanics had cherished.

How he'd wanted to be her first. For her to be his. However much he'd sensed that yielding that barrier would spell their doom.

Would it have been so much worse, after all? Maybe he'd been wrong trying to protect her, to shield himself from heartache. Would the past years have been easier with memories to cling to?

No way they could have been harder. Impossible dreams were as punishing to the soul as unquenched passion was to the body. He'd had his share of women since, but he knew to his bones that there was something missing from even the most heated sex when your heart stood apart and merely observed the process.

He'd had plenty of sex, yes. Been an attentive partner and made sure he'd never left a woman unsatisfied.

But he was still a virgin at truly making love.

The dog charged at him, butting Eli's leg with his head, then darting away, toward—

Gaby's house.

Eli took off running.

HE COVERED THE quarter mile or so in record time, every step a beat of the metronome of fear that he would be too late, that somehow the same people who had murdered Gaby's father would have gotten impatient and not waited for her to go. He'd thought she'd be safe because no matter what a bastard Chad was, he would never harm Gaby, not when he could marry her and control her land that way.

But maybe Chad's partners had a different game plan, another schedule. Maybe Eli should have been camped right on Gaby's doorstep instead of trying to expose the smugglers first.

In his mind, he could still see the burned skeleton of his mother's house. Still smell the ashes that had clung to his nostrils for months.

Still see the smoke rising from Frank Navarro's funeral pyre.

Please. Let her be okay. Please.

At the sight of the still-standing house, his knees nearly buckled with relief. He vaulted to the back porch and beat on it. "Gaby—" he shouted.

When there was no answer, he couldn't wait any longer. He charged through the unlocked door and raced through the house, but every room was empty.

The dog, however, continued to whine.

"What?"

The animal dashed for the back door, then arrowed around to the side. The momentary reassurance fled. Eli leaped from the porch and pushed through the stand of mesquites toward the rubble where her father had died—

And saw her on the ground, unmoving.

"Gaby—" He tore through the charred beams and fell to his knees beside her, yanking her into his arms, reaching to check her pulse—

Tears tracked through the soot stains on her face. Her eyes opened. "Eli?"

"You're all right? You're not hurt?"

"What?"

He began to thrust her away, feeling like a fool, but his relief was too great.

Instead, he crushed her close. Started to speak, then didn't. *Thank God, thank God* was all he could think. A world without Gaby in it, however distant, would be barren.

Then she slid her own arms around him, and he thought no more. "Gaby." Her name was a prayer, the beat of her heart the rhythm of his life.

Once they had created a world together, shared by only the two, a universe in which anything was possible. In this moment, they were children again, for Eli's only childhood had been lived by Gaby's side, those precious months when he'd experienced a freedom he had never found again.

His body craved hers, yes, but this was his oxygen, the closeness he'd experienced with no other. How had he lived without air for so long?

All too soon, though, the world impinged on them. The dog barked. Paco neighed. Birds sent out a last call before darkness fell.

Eli realized that they were out in the open, however near twilight was, in a land where visibility could extend for miles.

And tonight he had work to do.

His tension must have communicated itself to Gaby, for she leaned away from him a bit; laid one hand on his cheek, her eyes softening; focused on his mouth. "Eli," she whispered, and the simple sound of his name spoke volumes.

He wanted that kiss.

But not more than he wanted her to survive. Whatever she'd done to him.

He drew back. "I have to go." He glanced around them. "Why are you out here?"

She settled on her heels, careful distance between them. "I had to face it." She brushed at her cheek with one hand, smearing the soot. "I—I had this notion— Never mind."

He'd erected this barrier he longed to knock down. "Tell me." If he couldn't hold her, he could at least listen.

Gaby bit her lower lip. "My father always wore my mother's wedding ring and a lock of her hair around his neck. I had to find out if—"

She had always been the bravest person he'd ever met. "I haven't found anything."

She lifted a startled gaze. "You've looked?"

"I'm damn sure not trusting Chad Anderson to perform a fair investigation. He never even called in a crime-scene unit from DPS."

"He could have?"

Eli nodded. "Should have."

"But…why not?"

He wasn't ready to have this conversation. "There's a lot you don't know about what's been going on around here, but—" He glanced out at the gathering shadows. "I don't have time to tell you right now."

"Why not?"

He fought impatience. She was far too intelligent and insightful to be satisfied with a pat answer, but he didn't want her involved any more than she had to be. He turned the tables on her. "When are you going back to New York?"

She blinked. "Why?"

They were all but strangers, yet he had known her soul and she his. How much trust was left between them, after this much time?

"I can't say. Give me tonight, and I swear I'll come back and answer your questions."

Her eyes pored over him. "Just how dangerous is this?"

"Not much." He hoped the lack of light would hide the lie.

"Why should I believe you'll reappear to explain when you're lying to me right now?"

"I showed up last night. You didn't."

"I was at Juanita's."

"Leave her out of this."

"Eli, what's going on?"

"Gaby, I can't—" He stood. "I'm outta here."

She grabbed his arm. "Promise me you won't take any unnecessary chances. And don't expect me to like this. Or to wait past morning."

"I can't be spotted here in the daytime."

"Then get home before dawn."

Home. How sweet the sound of that. "Go inside and lock up good. Is your father's rifle still there?"

She frowned. "Yes, but—"

"He taught you to use it. Still remember how?"

"Eli, don't go. Leave this up to Chad."

He couldn't help his snort. "The day I trust anything to Chad Anderson is the day they put me in the ground. Now get inside, make sure that rifle is loaded and lock the doors. Keep the dog with you."

"Eli, let me go with you."

"Do not even think about following me. I mean it. Don't intervene in things you don't understand."

She tensed. "It's your fault if I don't."

"Please. Just give me until dawn."

She hesitated for a very long time, staring off into the distance. Finally, she lifted her face, and he could see the shimmer of fresh tears. "If you get yourself hurt out there, I am never forgiving you."

He smiled. Risked one stroke of her hair.

They both went very still.

"I'll be back before you know it." He stepped from her.

"*Vaya con Dios,* Eli." With huge dark eyes, she watched him go.

CHAPTER NINE

ELI SLIPPED ON THE shoulder holster and settled the 9 mm inside, then checked the ankle piece and adjusted the belted sheath for his knife. He'd never learned to like being armed, but some of the places he'd traveled, being a journalist was no protection. Once he'd accepted the necessity to defend himself in the midst of unrest, he'd made being competent at it his mission. He'd enlisted the help of the best warriors he'd encountered.

Right now, for Gaby's sake as much as his own, he was glad he had.

He donned the tactical vest with its many utility pockets containing everything from rudimentary medical supplies and water-purification tablets to the ever-useful fishing wire and extra clips for his weapon. Then he strapped on his night-vision goggles, but left them flipped up for now. It was nearly full dark, but an inevitable result of their use was a loss of visual acuity, along with a nasty change in depth perception. He'd make better time without them for now. It was still a week until there would be no moon. His eyes would adjust.

The smugglers wouldn't act just yet, though pinpointing the date could be iffy. Law enforcement was only too aware that the darkest night was the ideal time, so a savvy smuggler didn't necessarily wait until then.

Not that these smugglers had to worry all that much. The sheriff was one of them.

More than one of them, actually. He was the boss, following in his father's footsteps.

All Eli had to do was prove it. Determine exactly what was being smuggled and obtain proof. He'd sought to once before, of course, as a teenager, to find the evidence to free his mother from the former Sheriff Anderson's stranglehold. Melanie Wolverton had made mistakes in her life, yes, and Eli knew she wasn't innocent of involvement with the operation. But she had begun trying to free herself after her lover had had her son beaten within an inch of his life. He'd learned that, years later, from Juanita.

Eventually, his mother had died for her rebellion. Her death had served as a warning to all the others involved, Gaby's father included. But when Frank Navarro knew he was dying of lung cancer, a greater dread had roused him, and he had asked Juanita to contact Eli. How Frank had been certain that she could find him, Eli wasn't sure, but a man who feared for his daughter, however estranged, can be resourceful in his defense of her.

Gaby's father had made the long journey from wishing for her to marry Chad Anderson to being terrified for her to be anywhere near him. Thus it was that he'd sent for the very man he'd forced to leave her.

The same man who had spent nine years trying to forget her.

Eli tripped on a hummock of desert grass and yanked his thoughts away from how he'd come to be here and back onto his purpose, which was even more urgent now. Perhaps Gaby would believe him if he explained everything he knew to her, but he didn't know the woman she'd grown into, and he couldn't risk it. She had been forged in the fire of New York, its fast pace, its demand for excellence.

That was a different crucible from the one that had created him, fueled by deceit and cruelty, polished on the whetstone of loneliness that had become his refuge.

Gaby was no longer the wide-eyed dreamer he'd loved. Life had stolen that from her, and he grieved for it.

The loss was only one of many he was determined to avenge.

A voice ahead, a murmur, and Eli froze. Crouched and snapped his goggles into place. He listened with his full attention; then, once he'd pinpointed the direction, crept to the top of the rise ahead, angling for a creosote bush to provide cover.

There. Though the goggles didn't operate at maximum effectiveness at this point in the lunar cycle, Eli had no trouble picking out two figures ahead, lounging against the side of a pickup. One was lighting a cigarette, and Eli had to glance away as it flared. Only to the side, though—he needed to see a face.

He bellied closer, keeping the sparse vegetation between himself and the men. He sought information, not a confrontation, though he burned for the latter. Wanted badly to assure Gaby's safety by removing every last threat. Would welcome the relief valve of a fight.

But these men were only the tip of the iceberg. Chad Anderson and his counterparts were Eli's goal. Putting them away for life so that Gaby would never have to worry again.

Not that she understood enough to worry yet.

But he did.

"Six days," the smoker was saying. "The western route this time. Usual merchandise going south, boss says, but something special headed this way."

"Wonder what it is," his companion said.

"You aim to stay healthy, you don't wonder nothin'. Boss don't like questions."

"Yeah." The second man was silent for a minute. "But I don't get using the western route. It's slow as hell. Got to stay out of sight of the old man's place while his daughter's there, you think?"

"Maybe. But boss ain't happy about her hanging around, I know that much."

"Time for another fire?"

The hairs on the back of Eli's neck rose. It was all he could do to remain still.

"It's possible." The smoker chuckled and cast the butt of his cigarette to the ground. "But that woman's a fine piece, I hear. Boss got other plans in mind, maybe." He stood and walked toward his pickup. At the driver's door, he paused. "Like to see her myself."

Eli couldn't hear but a snippet. He had to find out more. He edged as quickly as he could manage to get within hearing range.

"Manuel—" the first man bellowed in a different direction. "What the hell's taking you so long?"

At the sound of movement just off to his left, Eli froze, his position exposed and cover too far away for the speed of the footsteps he heard.

"I'm coming. I'm coming," said a third voice.

Eli scanned the area around him, just as he felt more than heard the presence.

"What the—" The rustle of clothing, a belt buckle jangling—

Eli drew and whirled. Heard a commotion

behind him, just as the man reached for his own weapon.

Eli fired first, and the man groaned and collapsed as his own shot went wide. Eli revolved to face the new threat, but his foot caught on a small rock, and his ankle twisted. He struggled for balance but lost. As he fell, he felt a sharp sting in his left arm.

The fallen man began to stir just as two more sets of footsteps pounded in his direction. Eli managed to get on his feet and scrambled toward the rise behind which he'd hidden earlier.

How he would like to stand his ground and take them out, one by one, simply for the threat they posed to Gaby, the sly snickers that accompanied the innuendos about her.

It was three against one, however. He was a decent shot, but these were trained mercenaries. His odds weren't good, and even more crucial was that if he was downed, Chad Anderson would frame him for Frank Navarro's murder. He'd make certain that Eli went to prison.

And Gaby would be alone. At the mercy of the man behind her father's death. A murderer who was the son of a murderer.

Eli had no choice but to make his escape.

However badly he wanted to do otherwise.

So, just as the boy had once done, the man, bleeding and limping, stole through the night like a shadow.

Keeping the long view in mind, while desperate to return to Gaby.

Please don't come after me. Not tonight. Not ever.

Go back to New York and stay safe.

GABY PACED THE DARK kitchen, pausing now and again to stare at the horizon. She wished for dawn but was equally afraid of its arrival without any trace of Eli. She'd done as he'd asked, locking doors and windows and keeping the rifle handy, though to be afraid in her own home was an odd and unwelcome sensation. She'd experienced many emotions in this place, but never fear.

What on earth was going on? He'd been genuinely upset when he'd found her in the remnants of the burned barn, as though he'd seriously expected someone to have hurt her. Who—and why? The person responsible for the fire wouldn't care about her.

She'd contemplated calling Chad under the guise of asking for an update on his investigation, but she doubted her ability to continue hiding her knowledge that Eli was nearby. She'd kept one big secret for a long time, yes, years ago. No one had been aware that she and Eli had been meeting at night. But she and Chad had broken up over her visits to Eli in the hospital, and though Chad had soon wanted to make up, by then she'd understood that there was something between her and the half-wild boy, some connection deeper than either of them had ever experienced.

Chad had threatened to fight Eli over her, and she'd done the acting job of her life to convince Chad that her unwillingness to go out with him anymore had nothing to do with the boy they'd found on the road. She'd pleaded the press of her studies and had had to walk a precarious path to ensure that no one realized otherwise.

Chad had still gone out of his way to antagonize Eli at school. Fights had erupted a couple of times, but even though Chad had been bigger back then, Eli had fought Chad to a draw once and wound up on top the second time.

Chad had seized any opportunity to make Eli's life hell, but he'd grown sneaky about his torment, careful that no one could prove he was behind it.

More than once, Gaby had threatened to expose Chad herself, but Eli, though obviously frustrated, wouldn't allow her to do anything. Gaby had held her breath waiting for Eli to reach the end of his endurance.

But he never had. Instead, he'd distracted her, with kisses if necessary. And finally, since Chad was a year older, the torment had ended when he'd gone off to college.

She understood why Eli wouldn't trust Chad's investigation, even if Chad wasn't already convinced of Eli's guilt.

He never even called in a crime-scene unit from DPS.

Would Chad honestly go to lengths to frame Eli? Surely not.

She stared at the horizon for the umpteenth time, musing over what might be out there, what Eli was referring to when he'd said that she didn't understand what had been going on. Her mind slid to the safe-deposit box key, if that was what it was, and how she might figure out the location of the box it would open. She moved across the room, wondering if she dared turn on the lights yet so that she could continue searching her father's desk—

When she became aware that she could see her way to the hall.

Because dawn was encroaching.

And Eli was still gone.

THIRTY MINUTES LATER, SHE had gathered up water, food and a rudimentary pack of supplies from her father's medicine chest. Something must be wrong if Eli hadn't returned. Regardless that Eli had attempted to play down the danger to him last night, she trusted the truth she'd seen in his eyes. If he could have made it to her before dawn, he would have.

She had to go after him. She would take the dog, in the hope that he could help, and she would begin with Eli's favorite hideout from all those years ago, a cave in the foothills about a mile away, near the border of the Anderson lands.

But she had to hurry before it got too light outside. There was a lot of open country between here and there, and she didn't want to lead anyone to Eli. She would take Paco and leave Ramón a note that she was out for a ride and would care for the horse today.

"Let's go, boy," she said to the dog and shouldered her pack, heading for the back door.

Her hand was on the knob when she heard a pickup driving down the road toward her house.

A quick peek outside.

Chad. The road to town from his house passed by hers, yes—but did he have to stop so often? She stifled the urge to scream and instead scrambled to stash the pack out of sight. Suddenly, it occurred to her that if she pretended he woke her up, he might be less likely to ask to stay. She dashed to her bedroom, shucked her boots, jeans and shirt and donned a robe. She stripped the rubber band from her hair and mussed it, then ran for the kitchen and, with shaking hands, began to assemble a pot of coffee.

Just in time for Chad's knock.

Then she spotted the dog. And the rifle leaning beside the back door.

"Gabriela? You up, babe?"

She jammed the rifle into the broom closet and shooed the reluctant dog out the back, then walked as slowly as she could manage with her heart racing, to open the front door. "Is something wrong?" she asked, realizing as she did that his expression actually was very serious.

"Can I come in?"

She clutched at her robe, noticing his interested scan of her attire. "Um, I'm not really dressed."

One eyebrow quirked. "All the better." He smiled, and his thunderous mien lightened.

"I'll go throw something on, if you don't mind waiting outside."

Instead, he stepped through the door. "Can't I wait in here?" He moved closer.

Gaby backed away.

Chad frowned.

"I, uh, I'm starting coffee. Would you like some?" But she cursed silently because she didn't want him inside, in case she'd forgotten something. "Have a seat."

He looked as if he planned to follow her into the kitchen, so she held her ground, making her wishes clear.

"Okay." He spread his hands but remained

standing in the middle of the room. "Go ahead. Get dressed."

She had her clothes back on in record time, unwilling to leave him alone to wander. "Sorry. I didn't sleep all that well last night."

He tore his gaze from her father's desk to place it on her. "Me, either, unfortunately." His face went solemn. "Gabriela, I don't feel comfortable with you staying here alone. Something happened last night."

She was afraid he could hear her heart stutter. "What do you mean?" she asked as calmly as possible.

"There was a shooting."

Her mouth dried up. Speech was impossible for fear that he would tell her Eli was hurt or dead.

"One of my men was patrolling. He took a bullet in the chest. Couple more inches, and he'd be a goner."

Hope began to flutter. "I'm so sorry," she managed to say. "Did you catch whoever did it?"

His face darkened. "No, but I will." He paused, turning his hat in his hand. "I believe it was Eli."

She didn't have to feign her shock. "Eli? Why?"

"My man isn't awake yet, but I'd bet anything he stumbled on where Eli has been hiding. Rather than be caught, Eli shot him and ran."

"But you can't be certain."

His gaze sharpened. "Do you know something I should?"

"No—no, I just—" She lifted one shoulder as she castigated herself for blurting that out. "I'm only seeking to understand the situation. I'm uneducated about law enforcement or how an investigation proceeds. What sort of proof you require, for instance. All I know is what I see on television." She unearthed a smile, hoping to disarm him, all the while frantic to get him to leave so she could search for Eli—

Then it hit her that she didn't dare try now. Chad had all but told her previously that he had her under observation for her safety.

She had no choice but to wait until dark.

She wondered if Eli was hurt or even alive or had vanished again from her life. If she'd ever get the explanation he'd promised, so that she didn't wind up getting him hurt or killed if he wasn't already, simply because she was operating blind.

"Hey. Where'd you go?"

She jolted. "Oh, sorry. I guess I could use that coffee. How about you?"

He scrubbed his face with his hands. "Better not. I'm running on pure caffeine as it is." In that instant, he resembled the boy she'd once had a crush on.

"Go home for a while. Let María feed you and then take a nap. You can't keep going without a break, Chad. You'll miss something important in your investigation."

He shook his head. "No rest for the wicked, I'm afraid." He slapped the tops of his thighs, then rose. "I'll go home if you'll go with me."

If she'd ever been tempted, she certainly wasn't now. It was all she could do not to charge out the door this second. "I'll be fine. Papa had a rifle, and he taught me how to use it."

One eyebrow arched. "Armed and dangerous, eh?"

She gave a tiny shrug. "Well, armed, anyway. And I'll keep the doors locked, so don't feel that you have to spare anyone, including yourself, to watch over me when you're stretched so thin." *Please*.

He extended a hand and tilted her chin up. "You're special, babe. It's no burden at all." He bent and brushed his lips over hers.

Gaby steeled herself not to recoil.

"I'll check back. You stay safe, hear me?"

She managed a smile. "Will do. You go get some rest."

He tipped his hat to her and left.

She locked the door behind him and resisted the urge to sink to the floor.

Eli, where are you?

ELI YANKED OFF HIS night-vision goggles. Dawn was near, and he would be able to see on his own now.

Unfortunately, so would his pursuers. He could only pray he'd done a good enough job of covering his tracks. The thin high-desert soil was not like rich clay or deep sand; any imprints it retained were fainter, though easy enough for an experienced tracker.

And if dogs were brought into pursue him…

He was a dead man.

He was betting on Chad's fear of exposure, however, to prevent the sheriff from asking for help. Tracking dogs were a luxury this county could ill afford, and hunters hereabouts seldom used them the way their counterparts in wooded country did.

He'd walked about six miles, best guess, and his head was dizzy. Only a couple of hundred yards left, thank heavens. His ankle hurt worse with every step, but there was no option except to keep going. He wished he could make it to his cave, but with daylight fast approaching, finding cover was paramount.

Blood dripped down his arm, despite the compression bandage he'd retrieved from his pack. Thank God the wound wasn't bad, but he still should clean and dress it. His other supplies were in his cave, though.

As was all but one bottle of water he always carried in his pack. He'd skimped on drinking thus far as he'd zigzagged across this stretch of land, instinctively leading any pursuers away from his lair.

But his progress, however much he'd pushed himself, was slower than he'd hoped.

And his chances of returning to Gaby, as he'd promised, were slim to none.

If you get yourself hurt out there, I am never forgiving you.

His gut knotted with fear that either she'd believe he'd lied to her—

Or that she'd come after him when he didn't show up.

Stay, Gaby. Please don't risk it.

At last, the outcrop and its meager shelter hove into sight. Gratefully, he crossed the remaining distance and slipped into the cool shade with a sigh of relief.

He was too tired and weak from loss of blood, but he forced himself to stay awake to observe the horizon for a stretch, to be as certain as possible that he hadn't been followed.

Then he rummaged through his pack for water and his extra socks to utilize as an additional pressure bandage. He used as little as possible of the precious fluid to cleanse his wound, then forced himself not to guzzle the rest. He rewrapped his arm and wished he could take off his boot, certain that if he did, however, the ankle would swell so that he could never replace his footwear. He settled for elevating it on a nearby rock.

With a weary sigh, he closed his eyes and slept.

JUST AS GABY WAS ABOUT TO bolt from the door despite all the warnings shrieking in her brain, Ramón showed up. She rubbed her forehead and contemplated hiding in the house to avoid revealing her anxiety, then decided that, since she couldn't go after Eli for hours yet, the distraction Ramón presented would be a godsend.

She should eat something, but her stomach was too jumpy. Maybe Ramón hadn't had breakfast, and she could cook for him.

She poured them both coffee, though she wasn't sure drinking more was a good idea, and made her way to the barn.

The dog fell into step with her, tongue lolling.

"I'm sorry," she told him. "I couldn't chance Chad asking questions." Then she laughed. "I have no idea what I'm saying. It's not like he's going to question you. Even if he did, it's highly doubtful you'd give very good answers."

The dog trotted along beside her with only an occasional glance upward.

"Yeah, you're not much of a conversationalist, are you?" She sighed. "But I'm grateful for the company." She stopped. Bent down. "You'll help me find Eli later, right, Buddy? If he's not in any of the places I know, I'm scared that—"

She exhaled. "I'm seeking counsel from a dog. Beth would have a fit."

But Beth—and everything else about New York—seemed unreal.

Which worried her even more. She had no life here, no future, yet somehow, she was becoming entangled in something she didn't understand. Eli was in danger. Chad might *be* his danger.... There was more here than she understood....

Meanwhile, she had several hours to kill before she could get any answers.

Assuming she could even find Eli.

And that he wasn't—

No. Don't even think it. One step at a time.

Ramón peered out of the barn, and his face lit in a smile.

Gaby returned the greeting, grateful beyond measure that, for a while at least, she didn't have to be alone with her thoughts.

CHAPTER TEN

AS THE SUN NEARED the horizon, Eli shifted on the hard earth and groaned as his injuries made themselves known. His right deltoid burned—good thing he was left-handed. His ankle throbbed without mercy, but both were only irritants compared with his greater concern.

Gaby.

He could only hope that the levelheaded girl remained inside the woman, that she would not have tried to find him in the daylight hours for fear of being followed.

But the notion of her prowling around after dark scared the hell out of him.

She would remember the cave, he guessed, and go there first. But when she didn't find him there, would she range farther?

He'd like to believe that she wouldn't. The girl he'd loved, though, the one who'd refused to leave him on the side of the road, who'd persisted in visiting him daily at the hospital over Chad's strong objections...

His only hope was that she'd become such a city girl that the high desert at night would frighten her, that a darkness so dense would be too great a contrast to the bright lights of the metropolis she now called home.

He cursed himself for not delaying long enough to explain the stakes to her the night before. She was not experienced at prowling around in the dark alone. When they'd met as kids, he'd waited for her behind the barn and been her guide. The moon was only a sliver tonight, and there were so many hazards lying in wait.

He'd planned to scout the rendezvous point he'd heard about from the men last night, before the third man had popped up, but his priorities had switched. There was almost a week left to make his own plans to document the next illegal shipment. Discover exactly what Chad was into.

He had to manage to return to the cave he somehow knew Gaby would visit tonight—

Before she endangered her life by leaving it to look for him.

As the shadows of evening encroached, Gaby had spent the last hour peering out all her windows, seeking some sign of Chad's surveillance. She was grateful that he hadn't phoned to check on her, probably because she'd preempted him by phoning first. María had informed her that he had, at last, made it home for a meal and a nap. Gaby left a message that she was tucked in tight and planned to go to sleep early, thanking him for his surveillance and the peace of mind it gave her. She'd reasoned that if she kept resisting Chad, he'd get suspicious, whereas easy compliance might lull him.

She prayed her conversation with María about how exhausted she was would serve to encourage Chad not to chance waking her by showing up tonight.

Now, for good measure, she would lock up and hide out in the barn until it was nearly dark. She didn't want to risk piquing any watcher's attention by using a flashlight to locate Eli's cave; thus she couldn't wait until full night.

She was more than a little nervous about the journey but reminded herself that, thanks to all the walking she did in New York, she could cover the mile or so in fifteen or twenty minutes easily. Her eyes would adjust to the dimness, and she'd hedged her bets by wearing boots and her father's chaps over her jeans to provide more protection from the possibility of snakebite. She'd also dug out a rope to make a leash for Buddy, anticipating that keeping him close would be a sort of early-warning system.

If Eli wasn't there, she wasn't sure what she'd do.

But she couldn't do nothing. Eli could be injured or—

No use contemplating the frightening range of possibilities that might have befallen him. Gaby made her way to the barn, where she'd been secreting ingredients of an emergency pack all day. Medical supplies, food, water, batteries, a blanket, a sharp knife and her father's rifle, along with bullets… She'd done her best to anticipate a variety of circumstances.

Now it was time to go. She secured the back door as unobtrusively as possible and strolled toward the barn as though only a visit to Paco was on her mind. She would love to take the horse and avoid crossing the ground—somehow the thought of putting her feet down repeatedly without being able to see well was daunting—but Paco could make noise, he could hit a hole and he would require food and water himself. Better to leave him to Ramón in the morning, along with a note for Ramón saying she was sleeping in.

"Okay, fella," she said to Buddy, who wasn't pleased to have been tied up in the barn for the past hour. "Let's go find Eli." She shouldered the pack, stumbling a little under its weight, picked up the rifle and wrapped the dog's homemade leash around one gloved hand.

And stepped out into the night, glancing up at the evening star with a fervent wish.

However much he hurt me, please let him be safe.

AFTER WHAT SEEMED like hours, she was losing hope. She squinted yet again to attempt to make out the opening she hadn't seen in nine years. What had she been thinking, so certain that Eli would choose his former hideout? Now she was out here alone, stuck on the tiny ledge of limbo between a scary night and her fears for Eli, the prospect of returning in total darkness completely unnerving.

A hunch. Only a hunch, and she'd gambled everything on it.

Gaby forced herself to stop and inhale deeply, then blow the breath out slowly. Panic would do her no good.

But she felt like an idiot, banking on a memory and squandering the twilight on a trip she'd expected to end long before now.

How on earth had the pioneers managed? Imagine being out here with no idea what was ahead, far from lights and people and security—

At once it hit her how thoroughly citified she'd become, how dependent on 911 and cell phones and people and stores at your fingertips.

Remember what it was like, Gaby, those nights with Eli.

She closed her eyes, though calming her racing heart required a minute. The sky was too huge around her, the air a menace, every sound a cause for fear. She gripped the rope linking her to Buddy as though it were a lifeline.

Deep breath. Now another. Each one settled her a little more into the moment. The sounds she'd heard before, an accompaniment to the melody that had been Eli, one so overpowering that she'd noticed little else.

She felt his hands on her arms, his chest at her back. The slow in and out of his breath. *Listen,* he'd said. *The night makes its own orchestra. You have to respect the land, but fear is destructive. Honor the land for all it has to give you, for all it has given us. And love the night—don't be frightened by it. The dark can be a comfort if you let it. Stay alert, but relax. Even the animals will feel it if you do.*

Gaby's heart settled, and, as if he sensed the change, Buddy came to her side and sat down. She opened her eyes and bent to pet him, then realized that he could probably lead her to Eli's cave if she would take the leap and let him go. Quit clinging to him for dear life.

"Will you help me?" she asked as she petted him and began to untie the knotted rope. "I'm—" A hitch caught her voice. "I'm a little scared. I sure would appreciate it if you'd return to me very soon."

He hesitated as she untied the last knot, so she urged him on. "Go ahead, boy. Show me the cave."

And please, Eli, be in it.

The dog glanced at her, then charged ahead. She followed, forcing herself to stride forward as confidently as possible while still being wary of obstacles.

Then he disappeared from sight, and Gaby's heart clenched.

Until she realized he'd vanished into the mouth of Eli's cave.

As quickly as possible, she followed. Her pulse was racing as she contemplated what she would find, and she barely noted the familiarity of the rocks at the entrance and how it appeared to be barely a crease, nothing of note. She slipped into the entrance after first removing her pack, recalling how small the opening was.

"Eli?" she said quietly. "Are you here?"

Once inside, she kept one hand on the wall while she fumbled for the flashlight in the pack's front pocket. "Eli?" She recollected that Eli had shown her from outside that you couldn't get the right angle to spot either a fire or a lantern in here, but still she hesitated before flicking the switch, scared of what she might find.

She could hear the dog's panting. "Come here, boy."

When he did, her heart sank. If Eli was in here, she doubted the dog would have left his side.

She turned on the flashlight and went blind for seconds.

Then opened her eyes.

Eli was living here, she could tell.

But he wasn't here now.

Gaby sank to the floor of the cave.

And wondered where to go next.

HIS GERBER KNIFE HAD once again proved handy. With its serrated edge, he could cut wire, if necessary, so stripping off shoots of a mesquite branch to make an impromptu cane was comparatively easy.

In the late-afternoon shadows, he'd made his preparations, an inner sense propelling him to get back to his cave as soon as possible. His progress was slow and his footing anything but sure. The night-vision goggles played hell with depth perception, and becoming dizzy was all too easy.

Or maybe blood loss was responsible for that. The compression bandage had soaked through; he'd been reduced to tearing off a strip of his T-shirt and adding pressure by using his belt. When he got to the cave and could afford to use a lantern, he was going to have to break out the sewing kit he always carried and close the wound, if he could reach all of it.

Seeking medical care wasn't an option, not unless he was willing to abandon this operation without proving his innocence. He'd lived outside the U.S. for all these years, and he could do it again.

But what would happen to Gaby? Until Eli was clear on her plans and her relationship with Chad, he couldn't assess her danger.

This time, abandoning her wouldn't protect her.

He had no reason to think there was a future for them now, any more than in the past—

But he was sticking around, anyway, long enough to be certain she was safe, first of all.

And because he would not let the second Sheriff Anderson win. He wasn't a kid anymore, and he wouldn't be run off this time—

He'd traveled the world, exposing injustice to the light of day. Whatever his next step was, before he left this place that had haunted him for years, he would right this wrong.

And he would deliver Frank Navarro's last message to the daughter from whom Frank had let his pride estrange him.

IF SHE'D MADE A successful escape, no eyes would be watching. She could set the dog free again and use a flashlight to find Eli.

But there was no way to be certain she hadn't been followed without risking that she was wrong, and she had a much less certain idea where Eli would be, if not here. Gaby chewed her thumbnail and paced. The cave, once nearly as familiar as home, didn't feel the same without Eli in it.

It didn't appear the same, either. Back then, everything had been rigged from bits and pieces he could gather because he and his mother had had next to no money.

She smiled at his ingenuity; Eli had rivaled MacGyver of television fame with his ability to improvise. He'd had a pair of cargo pants, and his pockets were a treasure trove. Eli was a magpie—not the usual sort, distracted by bits of sparkle, but he was forever gathering pieces of wire and old nails and remnants of string. She recalled a ball of twine he'd assembled that used to sit right over—

There. She crossed to the little recess, and her eyes filmed. She lifted one hand, almost afraid to touch it for fear—

Real. Her fingers closed around it, squeezing lightly as if to recapture a precious piece of their past. She brought it to her face, sniffing it for traces of Eli's scent, that resiny aroma of piñon bark that always clung to him.

For a second, she thought she caught it, and she smiled, even as her heart hurt. *Oh, Eli...*

She clasped the ball of twine to her breast and closed her eyes. *Please,* she begged, a woman who had forgotten how to pray, *please keep him safe.*

The silence pulsed around her, and urgency gripped her again. Forcing aside her guilt over invading the lair of a very private man, she began to inventory what was here, what might prove useful in her search.

Because if she spent another night worrying about him without initiating action, she would surely lose her mind.

And she couldn't chance not being back at the ranch house by morning's light.

TWO BOXES OF AMMUNITION.

Three boxes of protein bars. Two bags of beef jerky.

A water purifier.

Four books, one of which she'd given him, *Broken Wings,* by Khalil Gibran.

A journal she wanted to read more than she wished for anything but to find Eli.

A very high-end digital video camera.

Laptop with solar recharger.

Eli, what have you been doing all these years?

A waterproof bag, light but lumpy. Gaby's hand hovered over the cord looped and tied at the mouth, as she wondered about the contents.

But she had already trespassed more than felt comfortable.

She opened the Gibran book and looked at the girlish handwriting: *To Eli, the soul of my soul, the beat of my heart. Love, Gaby.*

Sentimental prose, maybe—but truly felt in every cell of that romantic girl's body.

He'd kept it.

Sorrow seized her. Why hadn't she tried harder to locate him back then, and in the intervening years?

But she knew. *You'll make something of yourself,* he'd always insisted. *You'll go on to better things. You'll get out of this place.*

Not *we,* except during that brief span before the end. She'd used the plural all the time, but not Eli. She just hadn't wanted to see it.

Where have you been, Eli, during all these days and weeks and years that we've lost? Gaby caressed the worn cloth binding of the book, swamped by misery. What had Eli been going through, cast out all alone?

She knew what it was to be friendless, but she had the knack of making them when she wanted. She was not a loner by nature.

Eli was the most solitary person she'd ever encountered. Except with her.

The dog whined and trotted to the mouth of the cave.

Gaby whirled, quickly setting the book aside. "What is it, boy?" she whispered.

He nosed his way around the corner, toward the opening.

Gaby grabbed her flashlight and blew out the lantern. With her hand clasped over the lens so that only faint light passed between her fingers, she waited for her eyes to adjust, then she crept closer to the dog—

Who vanished into the night.

"Buddy, no—" But she didn't dare say it above a murmur. She clicked off the flashlight and edged near the opening, her heart thumping double time. She had to remind herself not to hold her breath, but she was scared half to death to peer around the edge. She held still and listened, every sense alert, but she couldn't hear anything—

Then a groan. Followed by the dog's whimper. As she eased nearer to the outside, she heard the animal approach. She saw him in the dim starlight just before his head butted her leg, so she didn't have heart failure as she might have. He trotted away a few feet as though waiting for her.

She inhaled and ventured the final step

into the night. "Here, Buddy," she called quietly.

He returned, but his reluctance was clear.

She gripped his collar, wishing she had the rope. "Show me."

Hunched to keep her grasp on the dog, Gaby moved awkwardly as she followed—

And nearly stumbled over something lying on the ground.

A body.

Eli.

CHAPTER ELEVEN

"No!" GABY FELL to her knees beside him. "Eli—" She grabbed for his arm, and her palm came away wet.

In the moonlight, it shone dark. Blood. Oh, God. She knew next to nothing about first aid. Her heart was a drumbeat inside her head. "What happened? Eli, can you hear me?" She bent over him, searching for where he was hurt, but his dark clothing interfered. "Eli?"

He still didn't speak. Panic tore through her. *Get a grip, Gaby. This won't help.* She tried to recall anything she'd ever seen or heard about first aid.

She felt for a pulse at his throat. When she got one, she took a shuddery breath. Thank God. But was it too slow or too fast? She attempted to compare it with the pace of her own, but hers was racing.

His seemed even faster. Much too fast.

"Eli?" She kept her voice down. Managed to make it sound far calmer than she was. "You're going to be okay." *Please. Oh, please.*

"I just have to get you inside, so I can tell where you're hurt." But how to do that? He was much taller and very muscled. She did Pilates, not weight lifting. She couldn't carry him.

Tears of frustration prickled. She had never felt more alone in her life.

Juanita Álvarez would be a better choice to treat him, but even if Eli hadn't forbidden Gaby from seeking the woman out again, she was far too scared to leave him.

It was up to her to save him. *Stop it. Now. You're acting like a girl. You're a grown woman. In New York, they think you're tough.*

All right. Okay. She chewed at her lower lip for a second, mentally surveying the interior of the cave for assets. Her mind caught on the sleeping bag. If she could roll him onto it, maybe she could drag him inside. Her legs were strong from all the walking, so maybe she could use their power and only need to rely on her arms to retain a hold.

She rested one palm on his cheek. "You hold on. I have to leave for a minute, but I'll be back, you hear me?" Tears threatened again, and she touched his forehead with hers, resting there for a minute. "Don't you dare die on me, you got that?" She pressed a kiss to his brow and rose. "Stay with him, Buddy." She patted the dog, then walked quickly back to the cave and slipped inside.

Clutching the sleeping bag to her chest, she soon returned and spread it onto the ground next to him. Wishing once again that she knew how badly he was injured, she finally had to steel herself to act and hope that the benefits of getting him where she could examine him would outweigh any harm from moving him.

For an instant, she lost her nerve. He needed better help. She was well versed in wines and literature and too many other topics that seemed completely absurd now. Nothing at all that could save a man's life. What on earth was she thinking?

You're all he's got, Gaby.

And so she began. As carefully as possible, she rolled him halfway and slid the doubled-up bag beneath him. She pulled with all her might to lift his upper body and hold it against her as she smoothed out the top half of the bag, then repeated the movement with his legs.

With every deep groan, she bit the inside of her cheek and persevered, torn between praying he'd wake up and that he would remain unconscious until she got him inside.

Then she started to drag him, painfully slowly, doing her best to avoid rocks and jounces, dying inside a little each time she jarred a moan from his lips. Her fingers were clenched so tightly on the bag that they were beginning to cramp, and her back was aching, but doggedly, she continued, inch by agonizing inch.

And prayed every second that she wouldn't kill him.

At last, they were at the mouth of the cave. She sank to her heels and let her screaming arms fall while she stared at the slender opening meant for vertical entry and tried not to weep at the impossibility of getting him inside. He was too long to make it past the slit that angled in an ell before winding into the main cave area.

She pressed her fingers to her eyes and forced herself to think. She'd never manage to get him to his feet without his help. She removed her fingers and stared again, measuring the gap. Maybe...

It was the only solution she could come up with. She felt over his torso for more bleeding but didn't sense any other wetness. That didn't rule out internal injuries, though.

Please don't let me injure him worse.

Once again, she considered leaving him in order to seek help, but her mind went again and again to his voice when he'd spoken of Chad. Chad's tone when he'd discussed Eli. There was no doctor for many miles, and if the county had an EMS, Chad would know of the call long before they could get to Eli.

She was lousy help, but she was all he had.

She sat down at the head of the sleeping bag and parted her legs on either side of it. Then she began easing Eli up to sitting as gently as she could manage, avoiding his injury and slipping her arms, at last, around his waist as she rested his back against her chest.

Then she began to scoot backward and drag him with her. With his length halved, she thought she could back both of them through the opening and around the edge.

Twice, his weight started shifting, and only the sides of the opening kept them both from toppling. Their progress felt as though it took hours.

But at last she had him inside far enough that she dared use her flashlight. As carefully as possible, she slid herself away and laid him back, digging her teeth into her lower lip every time he made a sound.

When he was settled, she fell to her back, every muscle shaking. She was nearly too tired to light the lantern.

But she had to. She made her way to her feet. Soon, a golden glow pervaded the cave once more. On unsteady legs, she returned to Eli's side.

And felt, once again, for his pulse. Watched his chest rise and fall. Saw the blood-soaked bandage around his arm, the ragged trails of red down his arm.

And prayed to be up to the task.

Then Gaby went to work.

SOMETHING BRUSHED AT HIS cheek. From inside the darkness, he reached for it. An elusive scent caught him, lured him upward.

Pain sent him spiraling back down.

Eli.

Who—

Eli. He swam toward the light. Shifted and recoiled from the ache.

"Eli. Please."

Little glimmers, tiny golden fish darting across his vision—

"Yes. Wake up. Please."

That voice, so sweet. So…lovely.

"Eli, come on." Aching. And…fear?

"Unh." He started to lift his head. Pain speared, and he dropped back with a groan.

"It's okay." Fingers, cool fingers on his face. "Please. I need you to wake up."

He blinked, and worried brown eyes greeted him. "Yes. Oh, yes. Eli, I've been so scared."

His eyes wanted to close so badly. Then popped open. "Gaby?"

Hands on each side of his face. A beautiful smile. Eyes swimming. "Yes. Oh, thank heaven."

He attempted to rise. The weight on his right arm shot instant agony through his body.

"Don't. Take it easy. I—" She chewed on her lip. "I cleaned it the best I could, but I'm not sure it's enough." Tears spilled to her cheeks. "I hurt you, moving you. I'm so sorry."

And everything roared back, the danger, the—

He bolted to sitting, and his vision grayed.

"Careful, now. You're still losing blood."

He shoved to standing and nearly fell back down as his ankle gave way.

"Whoa—" She slipped under his good arm and steadied him.

He tried to focus on his surroundings. They were in the cave. He glanced down at her. "You remembered."

She smiled. "I told you I would come after you." Then her face clouded. "I was so afraid. Chad showed up just as I was about to leave. He's determined to capture you, Eli, more now than ever. He says you shot one of his men." Her brows snapped together. "He neglected to mention that you were hurt, too."

"I hope no one knows." He felt light-headed, but he steeled himself. "What the hell are you doing out here? This is no game, Gaby. These men are dangerous. You have to get away from here—now."

She went rigid against him. "And exactly how do you plan to care for yourself? You're bleeding, and your ankle is hurt, isn't it? How will you manage on your own?"

"Same way I have for years. I don't need you."

He saw the hurt in her eyes. He had no choice but to ignore it.

But she surprised him. "Oh, yeah?" She stepped away. Watched him wobble. Lit with triumph when he winced and had to steady himself against the cave wall. "Well, I say you're wrong." She looked away. "You may not be happy to need my help—" Her gaze whipped back. "But you do, at least for now." Then her chin got that stubborn jut he recalled all too well from the hospital those years ago. "So why don't you quit being macho and sit down before you fall down."

"Anybody ever tell you you've got a head like a mule?"

Humor sparked in her gaze. "Dozens."

She'd been a remarkable girl.

She'd become a magnificent woman.

Her expression turned serious. "The crease the bullet carved is deep. I know next to nothing about gunshot wounds, but I'd guess it needs sewing up, and I don't have supplies to do it with. I have to get you to a doctor."

"No."

"What do you mean, no?"

"I can't leave here, not now. And I damn sure won't endanger you by being spotted with you."

"That's insane. You could die if I don't find help for you."

"You know there's no doctor within a hundred miles. I'm prepared, Gaby. In the places I've traveled, you have to be." He grabbed her hand. "There's a small med kit with a needle and sutures in my tactical vest. Middle right pocket."

She went dead-white. "I—" Her voice cracked. "Okay."

He saw the cost to her. His last recollection was nearing the cave, not making it inside. This woman was practically half his size, but somehow, in the dark, she'd been resourceful enough to maneuver him in here. As far as he was aware, she had no medical training and no experience with violence. In a matter of days, she'd lost a father and been confronted with both a past full of misery and a future that was uncertain.

His head was getting lighter by the second, dehydration, most likely, from loss of blood, but he held on. "I want you safe, Gaby. That means as far away from here as possible. You should leave, the sooner the better, but—"

One eyebrow arched. "But?"

He managed a glimpse at the bandaging on his arm even as the darkness encroached. "But I'm about to pass out, so you'll have to wait—" He started sliding down the wall.

"Eli!" She leaped toward him. "Oh, God. What do I do?"

He maintained consciousness, just barely. "Water," he croaked. "Need…fluids."

And everything went black again.

"I'M GOING TO KILL YOU," she muttered. "So you cannot die, you hear me? Not until I get

a chance, you blockheaded jerk." Gaby
checked the bandage once more, relieved
that the bleeding seemed to have slowed,
and lifted Eli's head again.

Water, he'd said. When she'd tried to give
Eli a drink from the canteen, he wouldn't
swallow. The liquids had backed up and
spilled over. She'd been scared to death he'd
choke.

Then she'd remembered a romance novel
she'd read once at Beth's behest and silently
blessed the author. She'd never wanted to
admit how much she'd loved reading the
book or how many more she'd devoured.
She'd have gotten endless ribbing from her
colleagues if they'd known.

But she was grateful now for more than
the hours of escape she'd enjoyed. The
heroine of that story had fed the unconscious
hero medication by taking it in her own
mouth, then transferring it to his. Gaby had
experimented with Eli and discovered that
she could control the amount better. After
some trial and error, she'd found a routine
that worked. It wasn't nearly enough, but
until she could revive him, this was the best
she could think to do.

Where was a good IV when you needed it? A competent medical staff? She'd never felt so helpless in her life.

Time for another drink. She sipped water from his canteen, then opened his mouth, massaged his throat and slowly fed the liquid to him.

His skin was hot, as though he was developing a fever. She was desperate for him to wake up.

She regarded the very basic medical kit from his vest. As if she were poking at a rattler, she trailed one finger over the plastic pack containing the needle, suturing thread, one pair of latex gloves and two alcohol pads.

With no anesthesia, he'd feel every stitch. She had no idea how he'd managed to provide himself with what seemed to be military paraphernalia, but there was a great deal she no longer knew about Eli Wolverton.

She was almost certain, however, that it would be a mercy to sew him up while he was unconscious, if only she could make herself do it. Since the furrow extended around the back of his arm, no way could he do it himself.

Oh, God. She was terrified. But this was no time for cowards.

Okay. All right. Gingerly, she removed the gloves. These were hardly sterile circumstances, and she certainly had no means to disinfect her hands, so the gloves would be essential.

She set up a makeshift surgical tray and had a semihysterical thought that she wished to heaven she'd paid more attention when watching *ER*. She removed a clean towel from the supplies she'd brought and placed it under his arm. She drew the lantern closer, then she sucked in a steadying breath and unrolled the bandages.

The blood was only seeping now. She used some of the precious water first to clean the worst of the blood around it. She would save the antiseptic pad until she was ready to stitch—or should she use it afterward? If only she dared to wait to boil water, but she hadn't brought enough for that and to feed him, too.

Oh, God. So much she didn't understand and so few options.

And she was so very tired.

But I'm all you've got, Eli, and you will not die on me.

Promise me, she sent a prayer to the heavens.

She squeezed her eyes shut. Okay. She'd stitch his arm first, then she'd start figuring how to get him to a doctor with tons of antibiotics soon.

With shaking fingers, she managed to thread the needle, being extra careful not to let the thread touch anything else.

Then, with a deep breath, she began.

Human skin was surprisingly tough, she discovered. She'd never imagined having to push the needle hard, and the little pop she felt nearly did her in. She swallowed back the nausea and sought to forget this was skin she was piercing, much less the flesh of someone she—

No. She didn't know Eli anymore. She couldn't love him.

But the girl she'd once been most definitely had loved the boy.

He shifted on the sleeping bag and moaned softly. To keep going required everything she had. Only the certainty that this would be far worse for him if he awoke pushed her forward.

Pretend it's the altar cloths Mama tried to teach you to embroider.

She nearly smiled at that, thinking of how often she'd gotten out of seamstress duty by wheedling Papa into telling Mama that he could use her help outside.

For once, the memory of her father was more fondness than bitter regret.

Eli started to roll away from her, and Gaby had to hustle. Without the ability to use her hands, she had to improvise: she rose on one knee and used the other to restrain his motion. Doing so required every last ounce of strength she had, but there was one bonus.

She had no time to think about anything but getting the second half of the stitches done.

He jolted violently.

Heart racing, she pressed her knee into his chest.

Eli bolted upright with a roar. Gaby fell back on her rear, and barely saved her makeshift surgical tray—

But she had to catch herself with one hand.

Getting dirt on one precious, irreplaceable glove.

ELI'S HEAD WAS GOING to explode, his arm hurt like fire, and he wasn't altogether certain he wasn't going to throw up. "What in blazes are you doing?"

But it wasn't hard to guess. Gaby glared at him while she guarded a towel like the crown jewels. She wore latex gloves, and she was as pale as milk. He glanced at his arm, with its needle and thread hanging, and he couldn't believe his eyes.

"You did it. You sutured the wound." With very neat, if not surgically knotted, stitches.

"Only half," she snapped back. "And now you've made me dirty one of my gloves."

"I made you?" He frowned. "It hurts like hell."

"Your precious kit doesn't extend to anesthesia. If you'd stayed asleep, it wouldn't hurt so much. Now I'm going to have to do the rest with you wide awake. Do you have any idea how awful it was to stick a needle into your skin?"

She burst into tears.

Even through his muzzy head, Eli understood enough to realize how hard this must have been for her. Gaby had always been so tenderhearted she couldn't even kill a fly. Somehow, she'd summoned the strength not only to track him down in the dark and drag him—someone who outweighed her by a good hundred pounds—all the way into the cave, but then deal with him passing out and still summon the courage to attempt to stitch him up. He understood from his own experience how unnerving it was the first time you had to stab a needle into skin.

"Come here," he said, and gathered her into his arms, even though in lifting the right one, dots danced in his vision. "You were the bravest girl I ever met." He brushed his cheek over her hair. "The woman has even more courage than the girl."

"I'm not," she blubbered. "I nearly tossed my cookies."

He smiled. "I had to sew a wound once. I have an idea how rough it was for you. I can't imagine how you got me in here or how you found me in the dark. I'd like to tan your hide for the risks you took." He leaned back so he could see her. "But I'm too damn grateful."

She regarded him then like the Gaby of old, her dark eyes wide and shining. "I was scared to death that I'd killed you—" Suddenly, she drew back. "You're awake now."

"Yeah," he said slowly.

She grabbed the canteen and thrust it at him. "Drink. A lot. I couldn't get enough into you before."

He registered his intense thirst, and not to drain the canteen required everything he had.

"Drink it all. I brought more."

He paused with the spout near his lips. "You are just full of surprises." Obediently, he swallowed the rest.

Then he glanced at her. "Pouring water down someone who's conked out is hard, isn't it."

"Impossible. You were wasting every drop."

His eyebrows rose. "So what did you do?"

Gaby blushed. Even by lantern light, her heightened color was obvious.

"What did you do, Gaby?"

"I…fed it to you."

"Fed?"

"From—from my…lips."

He stared at her in amazement. And, to his great surprise, considering his lousy condition, found himself viciously aroused. He focused on the lips in question and closed his eyes. Barely, just barely, he could register the memory of how they'd felt.

Then, despite the burn in his arm and the fuzziness in his head, Eli locked his gaze on hers and leaned close.

He heard her intake of breath, and he smiled.

"I—I need to finish up," she stammered.

Kiss me, he nearly said. *Or I just might die.*

But he reminded himself that returning to New York would be her wisest course, and even a single kiss would make sending her away so much harder.

He sat back. "You're right." He struggled to clear his head. "Let's get finished."

"I can't."

"Why not?"

"I'm scared to death I've infected you already, and—" She held up the one dirty glove. "I'm down to one glove and one antiseptic pad. I don't have any way to clean without waiting to boil water, and you've already lost too much blood. I'll have to go to the house and get some alcohol and—" She started to get up.

"There's a more extensive medical kit in that waterproof bag," he said. "Including extra alcohol pads, some disposable syringes, two vials of antibiotics plus two weeks' worth of oral doses."

"Really?" She frowned. "How did you learn all this? Where have you been all these years?"

"Long story. Get the pack, and I'll tell you what I can while you're working."

"Eli," she whispered. "I don't know if I—"

"What?"

She set her jaw. "If we both survive this, don't you ever get hurt this far from a hospital again, do you hear me?"

She looked so disgruntled and so damn beautiful he couldn't stifle his chuckle.

"That's one promise, sweetheart, that I will be only too glad to make."

CHAPTER TWELVE

SOMEHOW THEY BOTH survived the cleansing of the wound and the rest of the stitching. Gaby had to bite her lip to keep from crying, but Eli only sucked in his breath now and again, though she noticed his fingers clenching and his face going sheet-white.

He was brave, but she already understood that. His courage had never been in question.

Now all she had to do was to stab him one more time, and she was done. He filled the syringe himself, which was good because her hands were shaking.

"You've never done this before?"

She shook her head.

"It can be done in the arm, but I can't manage, and there's a risk of hitting bone or blood vessels. The better spot is someplace I'd prefer to be showing you under different circumstances." His blue eyes, damn him, were sparkling with humor as he gave her the syringe and reached for his belt buckle.

Torn by twin urges to cry and laugh, she nonetheless mustered the strength for a smile. He had to be hurting badly. If he could find humor, then so would she.

"Somehow, in all the times I imagined baring your body, it was never in this context, either." She stared at his well-muscled back and how it curved into his very fine behind.

Eli made an odd noise, and she glanced up.

To witness his eyes light with something very different.

Raw hunger.

Instantly, the powerful attraction between them roared to life, heightened by the knowledge that they were no longer kids but consenting adults, and sharpened by the danger around them and the deep and silent night. The awareness that they were alone where no one would find them.

Just as they would have been on that last, fateful evening.

"I swear I would rise from my grave to have you." Eli's voice was low and smoky, even as he shook his head. "No matter how sure I am that I should walk away."

Her hand lifted to touch his face. The presence of the syringe in her fingers snapped her back to reality. "You're hurt."

He held her gaze a few seconds longer, then turned away. "Of course," he said dully. "Go ahead."

"Eli, I—"

"Do it, Gaby."

There was much they needed to clear up between them, but first, he had to survive. She inhaled deeply to settle her nerves. To steady her hands.

"Either pinch the flesh between your other thumb and forefinger or use them to stretch the skin taut, then slide the needle in straight."

"I don't—" Oh, mercy.

"Gaby, now." Then his voice gentled. "Please. I know it's hard. Just position it, and I'll help you." He twisted at the waist, and she saw the strain on him. Realized that his color was bad, that the night had exacted a huge toll.

"No." She straightened her shoulders. "I'll handle it."

"That courageous girl grew into one hell of a woman."

His eyes were kind, and she understood in that moment that whatever had happened in the past, a part of her would always belong to Eli Wolverton.

"I'm not the brave one," she said, smiling. Then she bent to her task. When at last it was over, she laid the syringe aside carefully, removed the gloves and stood. "I'll be right back."

Then she escaped before she fell apart in front of him.

ELI SANK BACK TO THE sleeping bag, his entire body screaming for rest. The wound burned, his ankle throbbed and his head was pounding. He understood probably better than Gaby did that he was far from out of danger, but somehow he had to get her to leave him behind and go to the house. Then to fly to New York before Chad got wind that she was with him. Bill Anderson had been cunning and cruel. How much of the father lived in the son Eli wasn't sure, but he wasn't going to gamble with Gaby's life.

But how to convince a smart and courageous woman to abandon you and save herself? For one of the few times since he'd known her, Eli wished Gaby weren't so blasted intelligent. And stubborn.

He was puzzling over the dilemma when it dawned on him that she'd been gone too long for his comfort. He didn't think he'd been followed. He'd observed no signs that the smugglers had night-vision goggles—probably because this operation had been in place, undisturbed, for so long. But he and Gaby were not out of the woods yet, not by a long shot. He sat up, frowning as he tried to clear his head, then scanned his surroundings for something to use as a crutch. He wouldn't be much protection for Gaby if all he could do was crawl to her side.

Every vertical inch felt like scaling a mountain. He had to stop too often, but he persevered until he was on one knee with his good leg prepared to rise—

"What are you doing?"

His head snapped up too quickly, and the room began to spin.

"Are you trying to finish the job they started?" Her eyes were red from crying, her hair was whipped in a thousand directions, her clothes were bloody and rumpled.

He thought she'd never been more beautiful in her life.

"Pretty girl," he said stupidly.

She had her arms around him as she lowered him to the sleeping bag. "What?" She goggled at him.

"You're gorgeous." He settled back with a sigh.

She chuckled. "Okay, it's official. You're delirious." But her eyes showed worry. "I have to get you proper medical attention."

"Uh-uh. What you have to do is go back."

"I'm headed for the house as soon as you're set. I won't be gone long."

"No." His eyes kept wanting to close. "To New York."

Through the fog he could tell she rolled her eyes. "You're not only delirious, you're insane if you think I'm abandoning you like this."

"Dangerous, Gaby. Chad…smuggling."

"What are you saying?"

"Almost got…proof. One…week."

She gaped at him. "Chad's a smuggler? Eli, I'm all too aware that you don't like him, but—"

He managed to squeeze her hand. "Don't… trust him. Frank…murdered."

"You can't mean Chad. Eli, that's crazy. He's not that kind of person."

Her utter shock cleared away some of the daze. What did he really know about who she was now? He'd said too much. What if she tipped off Chad? "You're right. Forget it. Fever. Don't—" He grabbed her arm. Used the pain to keep him awake. "Don't say a word, Gaby. Not to anyone. Please." The darkness edged in again, but he fought hard to shake it off. "Let me sleep…little. Wake me in…hour. Have to get you back home."

"I'll be fine." She stroked his hair. "I won't be gone long."

"No!" Fear arrested his collapse. He sat up straight. "No, Gaby. Don't leave. Don't do…anything." He shook his head. "Damn it, need to be… alert." He was losing the struggle for consciousness, and he'd never been more afraid in his life. "Please, Gaby. Have to…explain…danger."

"Okay, Eli," she said, easing him down. "Okay. I won't do anything now. I'll stay here. You just rest."

"Promise…" He battled the muzziness, locking his gaze on hers.

"I can't—" He attempted to get up again. "Okay, okay. I promise."

He let his head fall back. "Thank you."

"Wait—drink some more first."

He smiled. "Like…other way…better."

He heard her giggle. Then he heard nothing else.

IT WAS THE LONGEST NIGHT of her life.

Gaby wanted so badly to go seek more competent help. She was deeply afraid that her lack of training would wind up killing him. His pulse remained too rapid—his complicated watch gave her the timer she'd lacked—and he felt hot. She'd crushed some acetaminophen she'd found in his medical kit and dissolved it in water, then used her previous method to feed the concoction to him. The taste had been horrible, but she would endure much worse to be sure he survived.

Wake up, Eli. Tell me what on earth you meant about Chad.

Chad. Another worry. If she was gone all day, how long would he wait before seeking her out? If he discovered that she wasn't in fact sleeping, what would he do? Would the search for her prevent him from his manhunt for Eli, or would he make the inevitable connection—and how would he react if he realized they were together? His interest in her was clear—well, at least, she'd thought it was clear until Eli's mysterious mumblings.

Chad a smuggler. How on earth could Eli believe that?

And that Chad had something to do with her father's death? The very idea was beyond bearing. Chad was far from perfect. He was jealous and could be overbearing. But…murder? He'd been so kind to her, all the while—

He'd have to be a monster to soothe her while knowing that he was responsible for her loss.

No. She must have misunderstood. Eli was delirious, after all. Merely fever ravings. But she couldn't get out of her head how he'd fought his way back to consciousness to warn her. To beg her.

She was so tired she couldn't think straight.

Eli's hour had come and gone, but sleep was healing. Gaby itched to seek out aid, but she was also afraid to leave his side.

Sleep sang a siren song. She'd just close her eyes for a few minutes, then she'd wake him up, and they would talk. Make plans, the most urgent of which was to get him qualified care.

But for now, she would lie down beside him and hope to recover some energy herself.

ELI CAME TO AS THE WET tongue lapped his cheek. "Gaby," he murmured, unwilling to abandon the dream he'd been having of her, naked and as eager for him as he was for her.

Another lick, and he smiled. Felt the presence beside him. Rolled over to cradle her in his arms—

Pain stabbed him like a red-hot poker. His eyes flew open.

The dog settled on his haunches and whined.

"Oh, man—" Eli reached up to scrub his cheek, but agony stopped him.

The figure beside him stirred. Long, dark hair shifted to reveal her face.

Gaby. Here at his side, as he'd wished for every day since he'd left her, however much he'd convinced himself otherwise. He levered himself up on his good arm and simply looked his fill while she was unaware.

Every line of her face was familiar to him. She probably had no clue how much time he'd spent studying her when she hadn't been aware, all those years ago. The woman who'd emerged from the girl was even more breathtaking, but it wasn't simply her features or her undeniably lovely figure.

It was Gaby herself, her huge heart. Her amazing courage. That fascinating mind.

Gabriela Navarro, woman of a thousand faces, some he knew intimately and some he'd never met. He wished, even more than he craved to clear himself, for the gift of time to explore all of them.

But if he didn't prove himself innocent, he would never have that chance. He'd be in jail or, more likely, dead.

The dog whimpered again, and Eli noted what he should have seen before if he hadn't been so besotted with Gaby.

Dawn was approaching. He had to wake

her and get her out of here. Now. "Gaby," he said softly.

She didn't stir, no doubt exhausted by the night.

"Gaby." A little louder. "Wake up."

The faintest of twitches.

He could tell himself that he was only seeking to be heard, but when he bent to her and nuzzled beneath her ear, he knew his motives to be selfish. "Gaby, love." He inhaled the scent that was not powders or creams or perfumes but purely Gaby. A lifetime would not be enough to sate himself.

She twisted a little, but toward him, not away, and he couldn't help the smile that curved his lips. *You trust me,* he thought. *On some level.* If only her conscious, too-discerning mind would play along.

So he kissed her, right on that tender part of her neck.

She hummed, a sweet little pleasure sound.

Oh, God. He was in no shape to make love to her and there was no time, but he would gladly hand over his soul to the devil for just a few minutes more of this.

Minutes, hell. He wanted aeons to cherish her. To explore every delectable inch of her flesh.

But morning approached, so he resorted to more desperate measures. Pressed his mouth to hers, and found himself sinking fast.

But he could also feel her rushing to the surface.

Then she was kissing him back, her body against his, her arms sliding around his neck, little moans issuing from her throat—

To end the kiss required every ounce of discipline he had. With effort, he drew away.

She made a little sob of protest, and he nearly capitulated. Instead, he lifted himself to sitting. "Good morning."

She granted him a sleepy, slightly pouty smile. "Come back here."

"Oh, sweetheart, you have no idea how much I want to." He scooted against the wall to keep from reaching for her. He couldn't help a wince.

"Oh—" She sat up. "Eli, I forgot for a second." She walked to him on her knees, touching his forehead. "You've got a fever. Here—" She looked behind her. "More water."

"Gaby. Stop. We have to talk."

"But you—" She registered his seriousness. Fell back on her heels. "Right. Chad and…my father." Her eyes locked on his. "The very notion— I just can't believe—not that you're lying, but—" She threw up her hands. "How can you be sure? And why haven't you gone to, I don't know, the FBI or someone?"

He sighed, fatigue settling in. "It's a very long story, Gaby, and I will give you all the details, but now isn't the occasion. We have other priorities." He indicated the opening. "It's nearly dawn. You have to get back to the ranch before anyone is aware you're gone."

"I can't leave you."

"You have to."

"You need a doctor."

He laughed without humor. "Sweetheart, I was injured worse than this in a third-world country without half the medical supplies in this cave. I'll be fine—"

"You've passed out on me three times!"

He waved her off. "We don't have time to argue. I'm covered for antibiotics, even if this required weeks, which it won't. I'll have to replenish the fluids I've lost, but I can capture my own water when what I have runs out. I have food. I'll be fine here."

"Then so will I."

"Sweetheart." He closed his eyes and prayed for patience. "What I can't do is deal with Chad or his thugs in this condition. If you honestly are interested in helping me, then keep them away from me until I regain some strength." He held her gaze. "If you go missing, who do you imagine Chad will automatically blame? If you thought the manhunt for me was intense, just wait until he can't find you. You have to go back, and you've got to do it now, when the light is enough to make your way but not so good that others will spot you easily."

"But—"

"It's true, and somewhere inside, you understand that."

"Come with me," she pleaded. "I can hide you in the cellar when necessary."

"I have all the essentials at hand. I'm not up to walking back to the house yet, and you can't carry me—or drag me. Not with so little time left." He resorted to last night's ploy, grabbing her hand. "Please, Gaby. Trust me. I'm trying to protect you."

Her expression demonstrated that it was the wrong tack. "I'm trying to protect you!" she cried. "I'm not the one who lost half his blood, who might die from infection, who—" Her eyes were bright with tears.

He caught her then, and pulled her into his chest. "I'm not going to die, I promise. And I understand that you have to do the hardest part. I wish like hell I could keep you here with me. I don't want you out of my sight, but I just—" He buried his face in her hair. "I have to stop him. I couldn't prevent his father, and my mother died because of that. Your father asked for my help, and I failed him. I can't fail you, too. Not again."

"My...father? Asked...you? Why?"

This was the part he couldn't get into now. He wished he never had to tell her that her father had been involved. "He was gathering evidence against Chad, but he needed someone on the outside. He was aware that Chad's father set the fire that killed my mother and blamed it on me. He was certain I would be interested."

"I can't take it all in. Chad's father...your mother. Chad and my—" Her chin rose. "He urges marriage, but he killed—" She shook her head. "I don't understand."

"It's complicated, and—" He glanced at the opening.

"We don't have time," she finished for him.

"Yeah. I'm sorry. If you'd go back to New York—"

"Not a chance." Her expression was somber now. "Don't waste your breath. I deserted my father before, but I won't now. Not even for you."

He nodded, aware that he had no choice. "How good an actress are you?"

She seemed amused. "Butter wouldn't melt in my mouth." She smiled, but there was no warmth in it.

"Good. Stay out of Chad's path as much as you can. When you're around him, do your best to remember how you felt when you trusted him. Act natural."

"You don't ask much, do you? So does that mean that the next time he tries to talk me into bed, I go?"

He'd remained cold-blooded up to now, but he couldn't stop himself from grabbing her. "Don't you dare let him close to you in an effort to protect me." With his good arm, he shook her gently. "Do you hear me?"

She stepped away and shouldered her pack, never taking her eyes off him. "If you think I'm going to shy at whatever is required to keep you safe, you've got another thing coming." She headed for the opening.

"No, Gaby—you can't—"

"I'll be back after dark." And she was gone.

"Gaby, no!" He yelled after her and staggered his way to the mouth of the cave—

Knowing it was too late, and he was too weak to catch her.

CHAPTER THIRTEEN

THE WALK BACK WAS EASIER in some ways than the earlier one, but in other aspects, much harder. She could see better, and she knew where she was headed, yes.

But leaving Eli went against every instinct she possessed. She was worried sick about his condition, despite his assurances. In most situations, he would, no doubt, be able to handle anything. He was strong and fit— she couldn't afford to focus on just how fit that rugged body was—and he was very smart and resourceful. From what she'd observed, his cave was amazingly well provisioned, and the cave itself was difficult to find unless you understood where to hunt.

But he was injured, and he'd been tended by someone who was barely competent enough to apply a Band-Aid, much less perform field surgery.

Where had he obtained his medical knowledge? His understanding of how to collect water in the desert? He'd been clever as a teen, but these skills were light-years beyond. Where had he been since she'd last seen him? And how did that square in with the laptop and the solar charger?

Most people had found the young Eli a mystery, but she'd believed she'd understood him better than anyone but Eli himself. This man, however, was someone with an edge and a darkness far beyond that half-wild boy's.

She lifted one hand to her lips and rubbed them softly, recalling his kiss. The thrill of awakening to his caresses, the rush of intense pleasure that was a forbidden taste of what she'd craved so desperately as a girl.

No man had ever had the power to really touch her deep inside. And now she knew why.

She'd been waiting for Eli.

Somewhere below the conscious level, the girl who'd wanted him to be her first was still there. A virgin of sorts, though she'd had other lovers. She'd had sex, but she'd never truly made love.

She spotted her house up ahead, felt the thread between her and Eli stretch and stretch, almost to the point of pain, and understood that, however far apart they were, it would never completely break.

Don't you die on me, Eli Wolverton. Don't you dare rob us of the chance to clear up what happened nine years ago.

To finish what you started tonight.

Just then, Buddy charged up beside her. "Oh, no—I wanted you to stay and guard him."

But she knew as well as she knew her own name that Eli had sent the dog with her for the very same reason.

Oh, Eli...

Her heart warmed, and she smiled.

At the back door, Gaby cast one last glance toward the horizon. The hours until dark seemed endless, the mile or so between the locations as far as moon from earth.

She sighed and let herself in. How in the world would she ever pass the time?

She entered the kitchen, began filling a dish with water for Buddy and setting out his food. She should eat, as well, but she had no appetite. Eli was out there alone, perhaps too weak to drink the water he should, maybe even now raging with fever, and here she was—

Stop it. But out of her fears, an idea formed.

She could cook. Make him a feast. He'd ordered her to stay away, but he was delusional if he thought she would abandon him in his condition. She would be careful, of course; she wouldn't risk leading anyone to him.

But she would be back. The first instant she had a chance.

She'd always been very good at reaching any goal she set. The malaise of the past few days evaporated, even though she possessed far too little information about what was going on around here. She must be cautious and very smart.

But for the first time since she'd answered Chad's phone call in New York, Gaby knew what she had to do next.

She made for the shower, stripping as she went.

HAIR WRAPPED IN A TOWEL, Gaby padded into her room for the underwear she'd forgotten.

Then she heard a loud knock at the door. A voice. "Gabriela."

Chad. Her heart jittered. *How good an actress are you?*

She rushed to wrap herself in a robe, wishing she had time for more.

Another brisk knock. "Gabriela. You're not answering the phone, and I'm concerned. If I have to break down and—"

"Coming!" She opened the door. "Chad, what on earth—?"

His gaze ranged over her. "You're here."

She clasped her robe at the neck. "You have this knack for waking me up. What's wrong?"

"María said you were sick. Thought I might have to drive you to the doctor in Alpine." He made as if to enter and frowned when she didn't budge.

If only that doctor would make house calls. And would keep his mouth shut. "I'm better now. Just…tired. A lot has happened. I seem to have hit a wall."

His frown deepened. "If you'd stay at my house, María and I could care for you. You wouldn't have to lift a finger."

The notion of María's tender concern

warmed her, and she could honestly smile. "That's really sweet, but I just need to be alone." She forced herself to meet his gaze. "I—I'm trying to come to terms with how my father died." She watched him carefully to see his reaction.

All she could detect was sympathy. Could Eli seriously be right? Was Chad a good actor himself or was he innocent?

"I'm doing everything I can to find his murderer, I swear it."

He never even called in a crime-scene unit from DPS. Confronting Chad about that was on the tip of her tongue.

But then she remembered Eli's reaction this morning. *It's a very long story, Gaby, and I will give you all the details, but now we have other priorities.*

She relented. Too much she didn't understand. She couldn't be sure of her footing yet. "Thank you, Chad." She yawned. "Sorry. Haven't made coffee."

He grinned and brought to mind the boy she'd had a crush on. "Can you brew enough for two?"

Oh, no. She wasn't up to small talk. She hesitated.

He frowned. "Never mind. I'm tired myself. Out late last night."

Searching for Eli? Fear raced through her, but she cautioned herself to focus on what she would have asked if she hadn't spoken to Eli. "How's your deputy?"

Chad's face darkened. "He'll make it, but he won't be using a pistol anytime soon."

"I'm sorry. I guess that leaves you short-handed." Maybe she could glean some helpful information after all. Even though she didn't really understand what Eli was after.

"Yeah."

"You look tired, Chad. Can't you take the day off?"

His expression was grim. "Not until we've caught Eli."

"What about requesting extra help?"

"From where?" His gaze sharpened.

She shrugged. "Oh, I don't know…DPS, maybe? What do rural sheriffs do when they need more manpower?"

"I won't have the state boys meddling in my county." His jaw clenched. "Anyway, we only have one viable suspect."

"But—" She'd hoped Eli had been wrong about Chad not calling for reinforcements.

He stared at her. "But what?"

Careful, Gaby. She summoned a smile. "Oh, listen to me, acting like I know the first thing about your work. Sorry. You just seem exhausted."

He smiled back. "Nice of you to fret about me." He trailed one finger over her cheek and let it linger at the corner of her mouth.

Gaby shivered, and his smile widened. "When this is over, Gabriela..." His eyes spoke volumes.

"I—I'll be leaving soon."

His brows snapped together again. "For New York?"

She shrugged. "I do have a job there, after all."

"So you're planning to go for good? You're ready to sell?"

How she wished she knew what answer would help Eli most, but for now, perhaps the best she could do was to keep things ambiguous. "I'm not sure. I have to wrap some things up at work if I'm going to take more time to finalize things here or..." She looked up at him through her lashes. "Or if I decide to return for a while." She sank her head against the door. "I honestly have no idea what I want to do, Chad." That was the most truthful thing she'd said to him. "I can't seem to think straight."

His hand stroked down her arm, and she forced herself not to flinch. "It's a tough time you're going through, babe. Just don't forget that I'm here to help you."

He bent as if to kiss her, but quickly she dropped her gaze to the floor as though she hadn't noticed and stepped back. "Thank you, Chad. I appreciate your concern. Have a good day." She started to close the door.

He hesitated, then backed away. "Sleep well, babe."

"You, too." Slower than she would have liked, she shut the door and only barely resisted the urge to lock it until after he was out of hearing.

Swiftly, she made her way to her bedroom to dress. As she withdrew clothes from the bureau drawers, her glance snagged on the top one. She set aside the garments and opened it.

The first thing she spotted was a circlet braided from grasses Eli had woven together for her one night as they'd sat beneath the stars.

"You ever consider what's out there?" she'd asked him.

He'd glanced up, longing plain on his face. "No."

"Why not?"

"No air to breathe. Can't stand to be stuck in some little compartment or some bulky suit."

"What if there's another world like ours?"

"One's enough." He'd kept his focus on his fingers as they'd worked their magic.

"What do you dream of, Eli?" She hadn't been able to stop staring at those fingers, either. Shivered as she imagined them on her skin.

"Being free. Leaving." His voice had been nearly too low to hear. "Taking you with me."

Her breath had caught at the notion.

"Where would you want to go?" he'd asked. He'd studied her then, and she'd had the sense that her answer was important.

"New York, maybe. Paris or London. Eli, just imagine all we could see. Everything we could do." She'd turned to him then, excitement jumping in her veins. "We could have a loft, and I could be a writer and you could—

" She'd stopped because she could sense his disappointment, like some test she hadn't passed, but she'd persisted anyway. "What would you like to be? Anything—you decide."

He'd peered into the distance for a really long time, and she'd tried to picture him in a big city. Had realized, even then, so young and silly, that Eli belonged to the land, that he required space, that he'd suffocate in all those crowds she craved to join.

When no answer had come, she'd placed one hand on his arm, caught by the notion that Eli was an eagle trapped in a cage, desperate to soar. She'd leaned her head on his shoulder, wishing she knew what to do for him—

He'd slipped the bracelet on her wrist. "I love you," he'd whispered, but he hadn't sounded very happy about it. He had, instead, seemed really, really sad.

Then he'd risen and pulled her up with him and started walking her home.

Gaby removed the bracelet from her drawer, wary that it would crumble after sitting in this dry heat so long.

But it held as she slid it on her wrist.

However far he'd traveled, she realized Eli was still an eagle. Still trapped, this time by the past.

He'd set her free, during all those hours spent together under the cover of darkness. He'd told her she could fly, could be or do anything she desired.

She understood far too little about Eli's past, but whatever she could do to grant him a future, she would. Even though that future wouldn't be shared with her.

She dressed in a hurry. She had much to do before dark.

TWO HOURS PAST SUNSET. Where was she? Eli paced the cave. He'd rested and eaten and consumed an ocean's worth of water. His ankle wasn't as bad as he'd feared last night, and now, with it wrapped tightly, he would get by. No fancy cuts or open-field running, not yet, but he could manage the walk to her house—

And he would, weak or not, if she didn't show up very soon. Only the knowledge that they might miss each other along the way kept him in place.

But not much longer.

He growled and raked the fingers of his good arm through his hair, executing a half pivot to cover the length of what was beginning to feel like a jail cell. For the thousandth time in the past hour, he checked his watch.

What the devil was keeping her? His mind was racing. He'd give her ten more—

"What are you doing up?"

He whirled and nearly fell over but recovered rapidly. "Where have you been?"

She recoiled at the anger he couldn't keep out of his voice. "I asked first. Your ankle's hurt. Why are you putting weight on it? And how's your arm? Have you had anything to eat?"

"That's four questions. Answer me first."

Her chin jutted forward. "A little overbearing, aren't we?"

He gripped her arm. "I'm serious, Gaby. Are you all right? Did you have trouble getting here? I should never have let you go out without the night-vision goggles, but they require some getting used to—"

She smiled. Pressed her palm to his cheek. "You were worried about me."

He couldn't help his double take. "Of course. Gaby—" He began to pace again, so he wouldn't grab her and never let go. "I've decided. If you really want to help, leaving is the only—"

"You've decided." Her tone was neutral. Maybe too neutral. "Just send the little woman out of the way, right? Never mind that you're injured, that you bled all over—" Her voice caught, and she spun away, shaking her head.

"It's not like that," he insisted.

She whipped back, her back straight, her eyes bright.

Tears spilling down her cheeks.

Then he understood. She was scared. For him.

"Don't," he said softly. "Don't cry for me, Gaby. I'm not worth it." He went to her, gathered her close. "I'm fine."

"Liar." She sniffed. Rubbed her face into his throat. "Eli, can't we just go away together? Abandon this place for good?"

"You can. You should."

"But not you."

He shook his head and pressed a kiss to her hair. "I'll be a fugitive the rest of my life if I don't clear myself. I'm tired of running, Gaby. I'm ready to come home." He paused, shocked that it was true. "Wherever that is. I'm not sure anymore."

She clutched at his waist. "Me, either."

With me, he longed to say. *Your home is with me.* But he had little more to offer her than before.

They stood in silent communion, united for the first time in so many years. Yearning filled him, and beneath it, the hum of desire, but however much he wanted her body still, he wanted much more with her. So much they might never share.

But for now, for these precious minutes, this was enough.

Finally, she spoke. "Can you tell me now? What's going on? When I saw Chad today, it was—"

He drew back. "You saw him? When? What did he say?"

She wiped her eyes, then sighed. "Sit down. Please. I brought you fresh tortillas and *carne asada.* You can eat while I talk, then it's your turn." She was all business now.

He wanted the pliant girl back, but she was right. They had more serious matters to deal with, however much he'd like to lock the world away and make love to her until neither of them could move.

So he lightened the mood. "Who made the tortillas?"

"I did. And the *asada*. I even brought you a *tres leches* cake."

He grinned. She'd remembered his sweet tooth. "So New York hasn't ruined the best cook I ever met?"

"Close. I hardly ever cook anymore." She smiled, but something sad crossed her face. "But it's amazing what comes back to you." Her gaze locked on his, and the memories of dozens of dark nights flowed between them.

"Here," she said, opening a towel that was keeping the food warm. "Eat before it gets cold."

He rolled a tortilla and stuffed it in his mouth, groaning his pleasure.

Gaby smiled and began to tell him about her day.

"LET ME GET THIS straight," Gaby said a while later. "Your mother was Chad's father's mistress?"

"Yeah." Eli's expression was bleak.

"When I was seven, I witnessed him killing a guy in cold blood."

Gaby couldn't help her gasp. "Did he know that?"

"Not until later. I couldn't understand why my mother put up with the way he treated her." Eli fell silent, his jaw working. "He beat her sometimes. Me, too, when he could catch me. I learned to stay out of his way."

"Is that why—" She glanced around the cave.

He nodded. "He wasn't so rough on her if I wasn't around. Something about me just set him off. I wanted to protect her, but—" He shrugged one shoulder.

"You were a child, Eli. What could you do?"

"Something." His face was hard. "I learned to pay attention. I followed him at night, sometimes. That's when I discovered that he wasn't content with a sheriff's salary or a rancher's income. He headed a drug-smuggling ring. The man he killed was one of his who got greedy."

"Are you serious? But he was the law."

"Yeah."

"Couldn't you tell someone?"

"Who? It was no different then than now. He ruled by fear. Not that I didn't try. The night you and Chad found me? That was his handiwork."

Her mouth dropped open. "That's who beat you?" Outrage sizzled. "Why?"

"I was young and stupid. I'd put the pieces together and decided it was time to use the information as leverage to make him stay away from my mother. I confronted him." Eli's mouth turned down. "He just laughed."

"Laughed?"

"Said my mother was in it up to her eyeballs. That he'd make certain that she went to jail if I breathed a word. As he pointed out, who would believe a kid everyone thought was crazy, the son of a whore, when put up against the word of an officer of the law? He didn't beat me himself that time, though. He wanted to keep his hands clean. He had one of his men drive me out in the desert and teach me a lesson."

"Eli, you nearly died. If Chad and I hadn't—" She pressed her lips together.

"Yeah." His chuckle was strained. "Guess I have to thank ol' Chad's libido. If you two hadn't been on your way to make out, the sheriff's problems would have been solved." Then he looked up at her. "I could never figure out why you decided to become my guardian angel after that, though."

She smiled. "There was just something special about you…."

"No one but you thought that. I still don't get why you did. And Chad has hated my guts ever since."

"Oh, Eli." She reached for his hand.

He tensed, then took it. He glanced down, and his eyes widened. "You still have it."

Gaby squeezed his hand as he traced the circlet with one finger. "I have everything you ever gave me." When his surprised gaze rose, she held it. "The arrowhead, the eagle feather, the sandstone you carved with our names."

Eli flushed. "Big spender, that's me. Nothing but the best."

"Don't make fun. It was the best time of my life."

He glanced up, disbelieving. "That can't be."

"You devastated me when you left, Eli. I would never have been ready to let you go, but especially not…that night."

He exhaled a long, low breath. "I wanted to make love to you so badly. It nearly killed me to keep my hands off you all those many months."

"Why did you?" She'd always wondered.

His eyes locked on hers. "Because you were always meant to leave here. To have more than I could ever provide for you."

"So you walked away, just like that. Decided what was best for me." Rage seemed to swallow her whole just then, and she broke their clasp. She stood, too angry to sit still.

"No."

"You always called the shots, Eli. Did that ever dawn on you that—" She halted, his answer at last sinking in. "*No?* What does that mean?"

"You never got my message, did you?"

"What message?"

He leaned his head back against the cave wall, seeming exhausted again. "Never mind. Water under the bridge."

"No, it's not. My whole life changed that night. I thought you didn't care, that I'd misunderstood everything I'd been sure was between us. I went to every place we'd ever been, checked any spot where you'd hidden a note. I couldn't believe you'd just walk away like that, not even after—"

His eyes opened. "After my mother died, and Sheriff Anderson told everyone I did it. Right?"

He looked dispirited. "Forget it. You should rest, Eli."

He rose to sitting. "No. Damn it, no. You were the only person who ever had faith in me. I gave you up to save you, don't you get that? It killed me to go, but if I'd stayed, you'd never have left, and you were meant for more, so much more. So when the sheriff threatened you, I had no choice."

"Chad's dad…threatened me?"

"I was careless the last night I left you. So besotted that all I could think of was you. I knew better, but I let myself forget that we could never work, and I was so caught up spinning dreams of making love to you and running away with you that I blew it. He was out checking on something related to his smuggling that night, and he watched us part. He had no idea it wasn't the first time. He told me that you were meant for Chad and I would not screw that up, that you'd be safe if I left you alone, but he'd rather you were dead than with me."

His eyes were bleak. "Reality set in then. You were on the verge of a very bright future. You'd entrusted me with your dreams of a scholarship, and I was sure you'd get it. And not only could I not offer you any of the world you longed to join, but now I posed a danger to you." His shoulders sagged. "I accepted that I couldn't have you. I went to my mother and begged her one more time to break things off with the sheriff because I was old enough to take care of her. We would go away and start a new life. I asked her to pack while I went to you one last time. She cried and begged me not to risk it. I told her everything would be fine. Then I went to meet you that night, understanding that it would be the end of everything beautiful I'd ever experienced.

"But when I arrived at our meeting place, instead of you your father was waiting."

She closed her eyes. "That's where he went when he locked me in my room. But how did he find out?"

"Sheriff Anderson. He had a man on me."

"What—what happened?"

Eli laughed, but it was hollow. "It should have been funny. Here I was, all set to give you up, but he beat me to the punch, telling me I had to leave you for a different reason, but one just as good."

"Which was?"

He shook his head. "You'd be better off not knowing."

She frowned. "Why?"

He paused. "This won't be easy to hear, Gaby."

"Eli, don't coddle me. Just spit it out."

He smiled then. "You always did have the courage of ten men." The smile vanished. "Sweetheart, your father was in on it. The smuggling."

"No!" She leaped to her feet. "No. He would never—"

Eli followed more slowly. "Listen to me—"

She shook her head violently, dodged him. "No—you're wrong. He was a good person, a moral one. I haven't a clue why you'd say such a thing, Eli." She was trembling.

"Gaby, calm down. I'm not saying he was a bad man. He never intended to be part of it, but he got trapped. They'd been crossing his land, that southwest corner that was always tough to fence, as part of their route before he was ever aware of it—but that wouldn't protect him from federal statutes that would seize his land if they were ever caught. And the ranch was struggling, so the money was welcome. Soon he was in too deep to get out, and when he tried once, Bill Anderson used you as leverage. So your father asked me to leave you alone to protect you."

Eli paced. "I guess I'd been clinging to a secret hope that we could be together, however impossible that was. I never understood the term *heartbreak* until mine did."

"Oh, Eli…I wish—"

His expression was grim. "I did leave you a note, though. I had to see you one last time. To be sure you didn't believe what they said of me, so I asked you to meet me. Hung around for two days after the fire, even though the sheriff had men everywhere hunting for me.

"But when you didn't show, I understood that it was over, that you'd finally gotten wise that we had no future." He shrugged. "It was for the best."

"I never found a message. I checked everywhere, but you'd just...vanished. Without one word. I was devastated, and all along you'd— Oh, Eli—" Her throat clogged with sobs.

"I guess the sheriff found it. Or maybe your father or—"

They stared at each other across the chasm of nine long years that never had to happen. The pain of it was crushing.

"I would have gone with you," she whispered.

Such grief in his gaze. "I barely escaped and only with the aid of Juanita. I left and went west and—" He splayed the fingers of one hand.

So much to absorb. Then one question rose above the others. "So why did you come back?"

"Your father. He sent word through Juanita that he had information that might free him and clear me. But he needed my help."

"What information?"

"I'm not exactly sure. We only met once, and he was very cautious. I guess he decided he could trust me, because he sent word to meet him again, but—" He didn't finish, but he didn't have to.

"He died. In another fire."

"Yeah." She pondered what she'd heard. "So why did you stay this time?"

"I have to. As I said, I'm tired of running. I've traveled all over the world, doing *The Hot Spot Journal,* and I'm tired of wars and famine and people starving. I want a home."

"Hot Spot?" She couldn't believe her ears. "The Internet journal, the guy who goes to all the dangerous places—that's you? You're…Max?" She glanced over. "The laptop with the solar charger. The camera." She was stunned, to put it mildly.

She'd read the journal herself, riveted, as many people were, by the manner in which the reporter—who was never seen on camera—brought to life the realities behind the headlines. How he put a human face on suffering, from Darfur to Iraq to Indonesia.

He'd been injured once, severely enough that his dispatches had gone missing for days—

"Where?" she murmured. "In the Sudan, where was the wound?" She extended her fingers as though she could somehow heal him.

He shrugged. "My side."

"Show me."

"It's not important."

"It is to me. Max just…vanished. For days and days. People were worried." She blinked back tears. "*I* was worried—about a man I didn't even know." She stared at him. "But I did, didn't I? I kept asking myself why I had to check for dispatches every day when I turned on my computer. It wasn't like me, not a bit. Not my thing at all, but—" She bit her lip. "It was you. Oh, Eli, how much time we've lost—" She bowed her head and swiped at her tears, aching for every day they'd been apart.

He gathered her in. "Shh-shh, sweetheart." He rocked her slowly, his body warm against hers.

She burrowed into his chest and gripped his shirt. "Everything changed when you left. I parted from my father with bitter words between us. The girl I once was couldn't survive after losing you—" She lifted her face to his. "I was all alone and scared to death. To survive, I had to become someone else."

"I'm sorry, sweetheart, so sorry. I wish—" His gaze dipped to her lips. His head bent to hers.

She closed the gap, opening to him and inviting him inside, needing so very badly to find that piece of her soul that had been missing so long.

His response was instant and electric. His arm banded her, brought her so near that they breathed the same air, felt the beat of the other's heart. Time slowed in that sacred space they'd once inhabited so freely together, as if it would last forever.

Gaby stood on tiptoe to get closer, wishing she could crawl inside him, entwine herself so tightly they would never be separated again.

She bumped his other arm, and his gasp brought her back to the world. She leaped away. "Oh, no, I'm sorry. I didn't mean—"

"I'm all right." He reached for her.

She moved back, but only one step. "You're hurt. Badly."

"Not that badly. Come here."

"Are you insane?" The strain of the past days caught up with her then. "Do you have a death wish, Eli?" Fury trampled over her yearning. "What are you doing, traveling the world, returning here, risking getting yourself killed—" She flung out an arm.

"Gaby." He grasped her hand. She was stiff at first, but patiently, relentlessly, he reeled her in. "Lie down with me," he murmured.

One quick shake of her head.

"Please."

"I'm—" Her chest was heaving. One tear trickled down. "I'm scared."

"I'll keep you safe."

Her head rose upward, her eyes blazing. "Not frightened for me, you jerk." She smacked his chest with the heel of her hand. "For you!"

He couldn't help himself. He started laughing.

"Don't you dare make fun of me—"

He drew her back against him. "I'm not, I swear. It's only—" When she went rigid with indignation, he buried his face in her hair. "You mistake delight for ridicule." He nuzzled her ear. "No one's ever taken my side but you. I'd forgotten how wonderful it is."

She relented. Clasped her arms around him and squeezed.

He nudged at her until she'd tipped her

face to him. "I am tired," he admitted. "But I can't stand to let you go. Will you lie down with me? I need to hold you."

He settled on the sleeping bag, but he never let go of her hand. Then, when she lay beside him, he rolled her until she was draped over his good left side.

A deep sigh escaped him. "I want to make love to you, Gaby, so badly I ache. But it should be perfect for you, and at the moment—"

She placed two fingers over his lips. "This is perfect. We're here. Together."

He gave her a smile. "Only the small matter of some armed men who'd like to kill me plus a few parts of my body that don't function so well."

Hers was the secret smile of a sorceress. "I can feel one that's working just fine."

Maddeningly, she was right. "Maybe…if you'd do the work."

"And chance tearing my needlework?" She shook her head. "I could never go through that again."

He studied her. "You would, though. If you had to. You're that strong. That fierce." He smiled. "That sweet."

"You're the only person—" her voice was nearly a whisper "—who's ever really known me."

He pressed her back against him. "'Speech is not the only means of understanding between two souls.'"

Her head rose again, her eyes wide as she recognized the quote from Kahlil Gibran. "'There is something greater and purer than what the mouth utters. Silence—'"

"'Illuminates our souls, whispers to our hearts and brings them together.'" He joined his voice to hers.

She cast her eyes down. "I have to apologize. Before I found you, I snooped. You still have the book."

"It's been all over the globe with me."

"Oh, Eli…" She blinked away fresh tears.

"Shh-shh, sweet." He cradled his good hand at the back of her head and drew her into another kiss, this time more longing than heat. Then he used his thumb to brush at the drops. "Right now, I would run again if you would go with me."

But she knew that to leave this unfinished would haunt him. "No. I would never ask it of you." The dark circles beneath his eyes concerned her. "We have hours left before dawn. Sleep, love."

"If you'll sleep with me. I dreamed of that often, what that would be like, to share a bed with you. After making love to you until neither of us could walk, having you beside me all night was my second wish."

"We'll take a rain check on wish one." Propped on one elbow, she stroked his eyebrow with one finger. She reached past him and lowered the lantern's glow, then snuggled into him. "I was never afraid of the dark when I was with you," she murmured as his big body relaxed.

"'If darkness hides the trees and flowers from our eyes,'" he quoted sleepily, "it will not hide love from our hearts.'"

Gaby remained awake as long as she could manage, feeling compelled to watch over him on this one, precious, free night. Tomorrow could bring anything, but at this moment, they were together, something she'd never thought to experience again.

Whatever was required to give them that chance to join their bodies as their hearts had long been bound, she would do it. After years of existing, she once more felt completely alive. Frightened, yes, and uncertain about what they might face, but—

Together, she thought as she drifted off. *Home.*

CHAPTER FOURTEEN

"GABY—" THE URGENCY IN his voice woke her. "Gaby, wake up. We have to go."

Gaby sat up, squinting against the light. "What?" She frowned. *"We?"*

"I can't let you keep taking such risks, traveling back and forth." He'd already shouldered a pack over his good arm. His limp was gone.

But he still appeared pale and strained. "Eli, it's too dangerous for you to leave here. Not yet."

"I've been thinking. I want us in the same location. Too many things could go wrong. We should leave before dawn catches us."

So businesslike. After last night, she'd expected—

"If, that is, the offer of the cellar still holds."

She forced herself to become the same. "Of course it does. But what's the plan?"

"Your father had hidden away documents—he told me that much. We have to unearth them. And two nights from now, I'm going smuggler hunting."

"Eli, you ought to be in a hospital. You can't—"

He rushed past her protest, handing her the pack she'd brought in. "I'd carry this, too, but I can't afford to have my weapon hand compromised."

She lifted her pack. "It's too light. Give me more." She could tell that his was stuffed full.

"I'm fine." He donned on a pair of goggles but kept the eye cups pointed upward. "Douse the lantern, then grab my hand. Give me a minute for my eyes to adjust."

"What are those?"

"Night-vision goggles."

"Where do you get all this military stuff?"

"Kill the light."

The tender man who'd held her seemed to have vanished. "I am not one of your troops."

One quick grin. "That's pretty obvious. I've never been in the military, but if you've read *Hot Spot,* you know I've spent a lot of time in the field, occasionally traveling with covert forces. I paid attention. Learned all I could." He paused in checking the weapon she'd just realized was holstered at his hip. "So I've got much better tools than when I was a kid."

He was all warrior now, a harder version of the elusive boy who trusted no one.

But her, she reminded herself. And she'd trusted him. That he was set on his course was obvious. If she were to get a chance to discover what they could be together, they had to get past this situation.

"Eli, we have to talk."

"Not now."

"Yes, now. I have a key. From my father."

His attention was all on her. "What kind?"

"Safe-deposit box, maybe. I'm not sure which bank. I found it in my father's things."

"Were you planning to tell me?"

"Of course."

"When? After you'd stuck your neck out to see where it went?"

"We've been a little busy. And you weren't in any condition to help me."

His stiff shoulders relaxed a fraction. "Always my guardian angel, aren't you?"

But his stare was deadly sober. "You're a smart woman, Gaby, and brave as hell, but you're out of your world now. If we're going to make it through this alive, you have to stop charging out there solo."

"You mean, act like a team? The way you're so good at?"

He was silent for a minute. Then he grinned again. "Guess I have to get up to speed on the new Gaby."

"Yes." She lifted her eyebrows. "You do." Then she relented. "But I see your point. I am a fish out of water. I promise to listen to your advice."

"Good choice."

"As long as you agree to keep me apprised and let me help more than you prefer me to."

He ran his tongue over his teeth. "But probably less than you'd like."

"Tough case, aren't you, Max?"

"Yeah." He paused. "City slicker."

She couldn't help laughing. "Okay, smart aleck. Lights out."

The darkness was sudden and complete.

Then she felt his hand grasp hers and draw her forward. Everything felt safe again.

"Hang on to my belt, so my hand will be

free," he whispered. "And don't speak, not even softly. If it absolutely can't wait, tug my belt twice, then put your lips right next to my ear." He bent and demonstrated. "Like this." His voice was nearly soundless, but she understood every word. "Walk in my steps as much as you can, and sweep this branch behind you to obscure our tracks."

He handed her a small tree branch. "We'll have to move a little slower. These things screw up your depth perception, and it's easy to lose your balance. When we get to your place, we'll stay in the grove of mesquites until I can be sure no one's watching. Got it?"

She nodded, then realized he was waiting for her to demonstrate her understanding. She stood on tiptoe and placed her lips on his ear. "Got it."

He put his mouth to her ear. "Let's go."

And swiped his tongue over her lobe, shooting her straight from worry to instant lust.

She couldn't help her gasp.

He bit the lobe lightly, then soothed with his tongue once more, trailing his mouth down her throat. "Quiet, I said."

She wasn't exactly sure how he managed the laughter she felt more than heard.

But before she got a chance for revenge, he tugged her into motion.

WORN OUT AFTER ONE LOUSY mile, Eli thought with disgust. He would never have believed it. Some days in the bush, he'd covered thirty, forty miles without ever taxing his wind.

He swept the ground before him with his infrared flashlight, its light on a spectrum invisible to anyone not also wearing night-vision lenses. Normally, he wouldn't need the flashlight for this short, familiar span, but he was escorting precious cargo. He couldn't risk a misstep that might injure either of them.

She was right, of course. He had no business stirring just yet. There was no choice, though. If she wouldn't leave town, he couldn't operate freely, needing to watch over her. Say what she might about being a team, she was out of her element, even if he were willing to expose her to danger.

Which he wasn't. She'd already dared too much.

He wished to hell she'd just go. Then he laughed at himself silently. After feeling that sweet body along his, after tasting her kiss again, he was ready for her to walk out of his life?

Hell, no. To pick up where they'd left off was impossible—both of them had changed too much. Though the draw between them was powerful, their worlds were incompatible. He was a no better choice than before. From earliest memory, he'd had no experience with the life that most people called normal. Once back in a sane existence, she'd see him for what he really was, a man who'd never found a place to stand still, to plant roots and let them grow deep.

Except here, with her. In this spot Gaby had spent her whole life desperate to flee.

His Internet journal barely paid his travel expenses, but money had never mattered much to him. He owned little more than what he carried on his back.

He'd seen most of the world, however, many astounding and incredible sights. So much of its misery.

And he'd had enough of it.

Not a great bargain, was he, all in all. He

should finish this and escort her back to the life she'd been meant to live.

But everything in him rebelled at the very idea of saying goodbye again. Not that he had the first time, except in his agonized heart.

He stopped at the forward edge of the mesquites, carefully dodging the long, needle-sharp thorns on every branch. Gaby halted, too, still clinging to his belt.

She wasn't even breathing hard.

He withdrew his pistol, thankful yet again that he was left-handed. That wielding it was becoming more natural. Slowly, he scanned their surroundings and spotted nothing.

He spoke in her ear. "Stay here. I'm going around the house to be sure." He let the pack slide off his shoulder and started to step away.

Her hand on his arm stopped him. He looked back.

Her eyes showed worry, but she blew him a kiss.

He nodded and wished for the thousandth time that he hadn't been wounded. He'd have had her under him by now, and they'd both feel a whole lot better.

Then he shut off his inner chatter and began walking.

GABY WAITED UNDER THE mesquites, the dog by her side, and tried not to panic. It seemed that Eli had been gone for hours. How long to wait, how to know if he was in trouble? She slid off her pack and bent with the notion of finding out if Eli had any weapons in his—

When she heard an engine approaching.

She waited a second to see if Eli would round the corner.

Then she grabbed both packs and took off running. "Buddy, let's go!"

She was nearly to the back door when Eli appeared. She veered toward the cellar door, dropped the bags and began to struggle with it.

Eli slid past her and opened one side, then tossed his pack down, followed by hers. "Come—" he ordered the dog.

Gaby whirled to head for the house, when he grabbed her.

One quick kiss. "Be careful." Then he slipped inside and closed the door.

Damn you, Chad, she thought, as she charged into the house. *Just once, couldn't you drive to work without stopping?*

ELI SANK INTO THE darkness and popped the eye cups down to scan for unwelcome visitors. So little light bled through the cellar door that the goggles couldn't gather much ambient illumination, but he was also counting on the dog's presence to dislodge any critters.

When nothing stirred, he flipped up the eye cups, slumped against one dirt wall and laid his head back, dismayed at how exhausted he was. He couldn't afford to get lax. Gaby might need him. He rested a minute, then opened his eyes again—

And realized that a faint rectangle of light was coming from the rear of the cellar. From within the house.

With the goggles on, the glow was almost harsh. He crept closer to investigate. Traced his fingers around the seams and felt wood above him. He pressed experimentally—

The wood lifted with a small squeak. In the gap, he could see across a floor. Over one corner draped what must be a rug. At the edge, he spotted Gaby's bare feet zipping along.

A loud knock. "Gabriela! I have to talk to you. Now."

Eli lowered thc trapdoor carefully, freezing as it squeaked again. Finally, it was closed.

He settled in to listen.

One hand on his weapon.

GABY HURRIEDLY STRIPPED off her clothes. Dust rosc in puffs when they hit the floor. She raced to the mirror and spotted the streaks on her face and in her hair.

Another knock. "Gabriela, answer the door."

She made a split-second decision and turned on the shower. She couldn't appear in front of him this way. He'd notice the kitchen light on and assume she was up, surely. He'd hear the shower running and either wait or go on.

Personally, she was hoping for the latter. She had nothing to say to Chad and no certainty that the night's revelations wouldn't taint her reactions.

And she wanted him as far from Eli as possible.

She started to step into the tub, then had a moment of terror. If she didn't answer the door, would Eli show himself because he was concerned about her? Could she make it across the hall without Chad spotting her through a window? If he did, she'd still be dirt streaked.

She gnawed at her lip. This covert stuff was complicated.

If Chad could hear the shower, Eli could, too. He didn't like her to be at risk, and nothing would be more dangerous than Chad finding Eli with her. She had to prevent Eli from drawing the wrong conclusion, worrying that she was with Chad and in trouble.

The solution, when it occurred to her, was so simple she laughed.

She entered the tub, closed the curtain and began singing.

ELI WONDERED IF HE WAS hallucinating at first. Then he shook his head and grinned.

Damn, he loved this woman. She was never what he expected.

And she certainly wasn't much of a singer.

Chad's footsteps descended the front stairs; her gambit had worked. He could hear Chad's voice and frowned, then figured out the sheriff was on his cell phone.

Eli crept closer to the cellar door, hoping to catch some of the conversation. Chad's truck was parked at the side of the house, and Eli was glad this house was small.

Now, if Gaby would just stop singing.

"You're kid—" Chad sounded surprised. Pleased.

The shower shut off, and so did Gaby.

"Holy—" Chad swore in rapid-fire Spanish. "Two loads of them? I don't know, compadre. The more trucks in one shipment, the easier it is for them to be noticed."

How Eli wished he could hear the other side of this conversation.

"Yes, I realize we can get a lot of money for these Asian girls, but if anything happens, they will stick out like a sore thumb. Drugs and arms are one thing. I never signed on for the sex trade." He was quiet again. "Don't you threaten me. Don't you ever forget I can shut you down cold anytime I—" Another pause. "I don't care about your money. I have plenty of my own now."

So Chad had a few principles after all.

"No, she's not gone yet. You stay away from her. I can handle her. She knows nothing. She's no danger to us. If she's still here tomorrow night, I'll make sure she's out of the way. You leave her to me."

Gaby could so easily get caught as collateral damage. Eli was with Chad on this one thing; Gaby should go. Soon.

"No, I haven't found him yet. You can't be positive that's who shot your guys. You've got plenty of enemies, Pablo. Don't tell me how to do my job. You get those trucks moved and get the hell out of my county."

Chad cursed vividly. A squeak—his pickup door? Then the throaty roar of his engine, growing more faint.

Eli exhaled.

"Eli?" Gaby's voice from above. "He's gone." Light flared as she opened the trapdoor. "Would you like to have a bath? You can't get that arm wet, I don't think. And I should probably check the dressing— What?"

He was staring—he knew it. But she was damp and nearly naked, her hair long black ropes down her back.

He handed up both packs, then, with difficulty since he had only one hand to use, propelled himself out of the small space. He made it to his feet but couldn't find his voice.

"Eli? Are you okay?"

He was dirty and weak and worried, but somehow, just the sight of her restored him. He trailed his forefinger down her cheek. "Yeah. No." What he wouldn't give to take her right here, right now.

He settled for her mouth, the kiss instantly electric. "Yeah."

Her fingers clutched at his back. She smelled like glory.

He forced himself away. "I'll get you filthy."

Her eyes locked on his. "I don't care."

He wasn't sure he did, either, but he also understood that life was short and uncertain, that anything could happen two nights from now.

That if he never made love to her, whatever happened to them in the future, something important would be forever missing from his life, even if the circumstances were much less than perfect.

"I'd like a shower, but you're right. Let me bathe, then you can check the dressing. Then—" He let his look speak for him.

Faint color stained her cheeks, but her

gaze answered back. Her smile was lazy and beautiful and just a little wicked. "Oh, yeah," she echoed. Long and low and sultry.

Eli's answering groan was heartfelt.

GABY STARTED THE WASHER running, putting in Eli's garments with hers. Such a stupid, sophomoric thing to gain pleasure from, tracing a finger over the collar of his shirt, seeing his jeans mix with hers. She was not Betty Crocker or June Cleaver, hadn't been remotely domestic in years. If she'd ever had a long-term man in her life, she would have demanded that he share all the house-keeping and cooking chores because she was so wrapped up in her career and had always assumed hers would be as important as that of any man she'd live with.

Somehow, though, that man had never appeared. She'd dated a lawyer and an artist, a writer and an accountant, one politician and a couple of actors. None of them had stuck, and she'd told herself she was in no hurry.

She'd been dead wrong. No one had made the cut because none of them was Eli. As simple as that, and as complicated.

How could their lives mesh now? The

man millions called Max traveled light; a companion would only slow him down, even if she were the type for hair-raising adventure, for roughing it.

Which she most definitely was not. But neither could she picture him in Manhattan. His reporting was brilliant, and he could bring those same insights to stories on the domestic front or crime reporting or any of a host of possibilities—

But Eli was a creature of air and space and light. The eagle would die in the zoo that was New York.

She punched the starter button on the washer and shook off her maudlin thoughts. They were in the same place now, and she was not about to waste a second of their time.

A little shiver ran through her at the memory of the heat in his eyes. He wanted her, and God knows she wanted him. She should be responsible and discourage him until he was better—

But they were together now. Who could say what tomorrow would bring?

Eager not to be apart any longer, she approached the bathroom door, realizing that she didn't hear any splashing. "Eli?"

No response. What if the journey drained him too much and he'd passed out again or—

"Eli, are you all right?"

Still nothing. She eased the door open, just a fraction.

His head lay against the back of the old clawfoot tub. With a pounding heart, she approached, hesitant to violate his privacy, hoping he was only resting—

His chest rose slowly. Gaby tiptoed closer. His eyes were shut. Weariness was carved into his features. His injured arm lay propped on a towel at the edge of the tub. She had the urge to place a pillow beneath his head to make him more comfortable, but—

Lord have mercy. What a body he had. She shouldn't have been ogling, of course, but she'd have to be made of sterner stuff to resist. The girl she once was had been very curious about what had been beneath those T-shirts and jeans, but all she'd been able to gather had come from heavy make-out sessions where Eli would call a halt before things got out of hand.

The boy had quite definitely become a man, broad, muscled chest now covered with black hair from nipple to nipple, narrowing down in the arrow every woman knew to follow toward—

Oh, Lordy.

"Obviously, I'm not dead yet."

His voice jolted her. "I'm sorry. I shouldn't—"

"Feel free. Just loosen the tie of that robe while you're at it."

She heard the smile. The tease.

She glanced over. And registered the heat. Felt it shimmer inside her. "We should be smart. You're not well. We should wait."

"I disagree." He stood, and water sluiced down his body, outlining every muscle, every angle.

She'd never seen anything like him. He had nothing in common with the buffed and toned men of her world or the male models in magazines or on billboards.

Eli wasn't pretty. He was man with a capital *M*. Hard and lean and the best-looking thing she'd ever laid eyes on.

Then she spotted the scars. "Oh, Eli." She stepped forward, traced her fingers over the puckered hole at his side, the ridged white line on his thigh. Bent and touched her lips to each one as if she could heal the old hurts.

Eli gasped. Dug his fingers into her hair.

She trailed a line of kisses up to his hip, brushed her hair against the hard evidence of his desire. Turned her face and slicked her tongue over him.

"Sweet mother of—" Eli jerked away. Snagged a towel.

"You don't like it?" she asked innocently, loving the strain on his face. She rose to her toes and swirled her tongue over one of his nipples.

"Get away from me, woman." His voice was low and just the slightest bit unsteady.

"No." She slid her hands up his sides. Caught the towel and threw it behind her. Smiled up at him and smiled. "This time, you won't make me stop. Not anymore."

Blue eyes blazed. "I don't want you to. I'd chew my way through razor wire to have you, Gaby." He kissed her in a manner that left no room for misunderstanding. "But I'd like a chance to touch you, too. Another three seconds of that, and it would all be over."

His body was tense. Quivering. "Are you

certain about this, Eli? I refuse to be a part of hurting you."

He emerged from the tub, grabbed her wrist and towed her into the bedroom. "Yes, I'm sure."

"But we have to change the bandage—"

"Screw the bandage." Then his mouth was on hers, his hand untying the belt of her robe, then sweeping the garment from her shoulders.

With impressive strength, he drew her to him, flesh to flesh from chest to thigh. He inserted one leg between hers, and she writhed against him, moaning softly as she dug her fingers into his hair.

He back away and suddenly. "Hold on—"

"What do you mean, hold on?" She had to stifle a scream.

She took consolation from the fact that his chest was heaving, too. That his eyes were steel-melting hot.

"I've waited half my life to see you naked. I'm not rushing." His gaze traveled over her, and she felt burned by every inch of his progress.

Her nipples tightened, and little shocks spilled through her. "That's enough." This time she grabbed him. Plastered herself to his chest. "Time's up." She slanted her lips over his.

"Damn it." He closed his eyes. "I'm not carrying any condoms. I don't have any diseases, but—"

"Me, either. And I'm on the Pill." She clenched her fingers in his hair. "So shut up and kiss me."

He laughed against her mouth, then groaned. "I've dreamed of this since I was sixteen." Then he took her under.

She gladly drowned in the swell, the waves of emotion swamping her, the sheer miracle of being here with him, their bodies together after so long—

Somehow they made it to the mattress, though they were never more than a breath apart.

"Lie back. Let me, so we don't hurt your arm." She began with his throat, kissing her way down his body.

"No—" He hauled her up, had her straddle his chest. Used his mouth to carve a devastating path up one thigh until he reached the heart of her.

"Eli—" She arched in bliss, grasped his

hair, trying not to tear it from the roots. Her mind flew somewhere beyond the stars.

She caught herself on the headboard, trembling as she struggled to breathe, to think.

Rapturous as the sensations were, she needed him, the full communion of body to body. She made her way down the front of him, poised and waiting as his big hand splayed across her hip.

His face showed the strain of holding himself back.

"Eli."

His eyes opened.

"It doesn't matter what happened. All that matters is us. This."

"This can only be now." His hand tightened on her. "I have nothing to offer you. I don't fit in your life."

"I don't fit in yours. At the moment, I don't care."

"You should, but—" He guided her lower, grazed against her tender flesh.

She sucked in a breath. Started to slide onto him.

He halted her. "I will keep you safe, Gaby, I swear it."

"You always did." She gazed into his eyes.

"Come inside me, Eli. Make us one. Take that last step."

He slipped into her with velvety tenderness, so slow and exquisitely that she wanted to weep for all the times he'd cared for her, watched over her.

"Don't cry, love." He brushed at her tears and pulled her head down, but his eyes were damp, too.

Their lips met, and the kiss was both heat and unbearable sweetness as that final click sounded for them both, the key in the lock, opening the door to a treasure they'd glimpsed but never dared claim.

Then they began to move, two hearts soaring, flying, souls mating as everything else ceased to matter. Power and beauty shimmered in the air, wrapping them in the warmth so long denied them. Together at last. United after suffering so long apart.

Love lifted them up, let them forget. Let them revel. There was ecstasy, there was comfort…there was safety. They drifted to earth, curled together in an oddly innocent slumber.

And in that sacred space, were, for a precious moment in time, wholly one.

CHAPTER FIFTEEN

ELI OPENED HIS EYES to sunshine. And smiled as memories flooded in.

Sable hair draped over his chest. Gaby slept, boneless as an infant. There were many things they should do, steps they needed to take.

Not one of them as compelling as lingering in a moment he'd dreamed of but never expected to experience.

He'd made a terrible mistake. Leaving her this time would definitely kill him. However incredible he'd imagined making love to her would be—

He hadn't even begun to guess at the miracle of it. Not once in his life had he ever felt so complete. The closest he'd ever come was all the hours he'd spent with her as kids, talking about everything under the sun. He'd loved her, that he'd never doubted, and she'd loved him.

But having her in his arms, being inside her, seeing her eyes shine with the same magic he was feeling…

He would be half a man without her.

Less than half. He'd be howling-at-the-moon crazy.

Dear God. He'd opened Pandora's box, and what lay inside scared him as nothing ever had.

He clutched at Gaby with his good arm and ignored the throbbing of his wound. He stared at the ceiling and beyond it to the desert his life had been. The wasteland it would become when she was gone.

He'd sell his soul to keep her, but the odds of that weren't good, not if she used that brilliant brain of hers. She might not—her heart was huge, outsized for her small body—so it was up to him to make certain that she did. Nothing in this world was more critical than protecting her.

Eli pressed a kiss to her hair and tried to switch his thoughts to the hours ahead of them and what must be accomplished. First, he had to gain what strength he could. Gaby slumbered on, and he should join her. Gather himself for the battle ahead.

But instead, for long moments, he contemplated a future much bleaker than his past, holding tightly to the woman who had always been the color in his gray world, not wanting to miss a second of the time they had together.

But eventually, his injury and the long nights without rest caught up to him.

And Eli slept.

GABY STIRRED, SUFFUSED with a sense of well-being. She rolled her head to the side and remembered why.

And smiled.

Every cell in her body was doing a happy dance. Singing the "Hallelujah Chorus." If that was how Eli made love when he was injured, just imagine...

She shivered at the delicious notion of it. God willing, she'd get the chance to compare and contrast.

She emerged from the bed carefully so he would sleep. Dark circles beneath his eyes demonstrated the toll of his injuries and the strain he'd been under. How he'd ever summoned the energy to make love to her, much less such astonishing love—wow.

She must leave him alone, however badly she longed to awaken him with a leisurely, delicious journey over every inch of that amazing body.

Let him be, you greedy witch. Despite how serious their circumstances were, Gaby couldn't help grinning. She'd never been insatiable before, but oh, baby, baby…

Before her self-control faltered completely, she snatched some clothes and made her way from the room. Eli needed rest first and food second. She would get to work in the kitchen and keep her hands to herself.

For now, at least. But when he recovered…

Another shiver trickled over her.

Eli. Yum.

THE PHONE RANG, and she pounced on it. "Hello?"

"You okay, Gabriela?"

Chad. "Oh—sure. Fine. Why?"

"Something wrong with your voice? You're so quiet."

If only her father had sprung for a portable phone. Gaby retreated into the far corner of the living room and curled her back. Attempted a feint. "I can't tell any difference. Maybe the phone line?"

"Maybe. I'll call María to check our phone."

Come on, come on, she urged silently. *Let's get finished before Eli wakes.* But to Chad she only said, "What's up?"

"Just making sure you're okay. You didn't answer the door this morning."

"Chad, you don't have to check on me every day." She struggled to keep the annoyance from her voice. With Eli here, it was imperative not to arouse his suspicions. "I was probably in the shower."

"I wondered." A small chuckle. "I could have sworn I heard you singing."

She uttered mute thanks her gamble had worked. "Don't guess I should hold out hopes for that recording contract, huh?"

A short laugh. "I plead the Fifth."

This was Chad, the charming boy she'd once been crazy about. How could he possibly have—

But she couldn't forget the menace in his eyes when he'd battled Eli as teens. When he'd promised that Eli would pay for her father's murder. "I might be gone some the next few days." Abruptly, she decided.

"Where?"

She closed her eyes. Fought the urge to say *none of your business.* "I need to clear my head. Figure out what I really want. I have a lot of vacation time built up, so I thought I might head over to Alpine and Marfa. Fort Davis. Maybe even check out El Paso and stay a night or two."

"Don't cross the border. Things have gotten nasty the past few years. I'd rather you didn't go to El Paso, actually. Kidnappers are operating out of all the border towns."

"They're after rich *gringas,* Chad, not Latinas." *And don't order me around,* she was dying to say but didn't. "Nobody's paying a ransom for me."

"I would." His voice was husky with the ring of true emotion. "I'd do anything to protect you, Gabriela."

He sounded so sincere that she was tempted to believe him. "That's very sweet." If he knew she was harboring Eli, his tune would no doubt be quite different.

"I'm not sweet." An edge crept in. "I protect what's important to me. Damn it, Gabriela, how long are you going to keep me hanging? You know I care about you."

Me? Or my land? "Chad, I—" She bit her lip. "I wish I could think straight. If I hadn't left my father on such bad terms, maybe this decision wouldn't be so difficult, but I have a life in New York, and I worked very hard to get where I am. I just received an important promotion. My course was set, but now…here…so much to deal with. So many memories and regrets—"

"Where do I fit in that?" he asked. "Am I a memory…or a regret?"

"You're some of both." That, like her turmoil, was honest.

"I want to be your future. I won't lie about that."

"Chad—"

"Don't. I'm not asking you to choose, not yet. But I'm going to be straight with you. I'll buy your land, Gabriela, if New York is what you want, but I won't kid you. I'd rather have you. I'm going to find Eli Wolverton and wrap up your father's murder. Once that's done, maybe you'll be able to figure things out, without that cloud hanging over your head." He paused. Exhaled sharply. "So, no, I don't like the idea of you wandering around with a murderer on the loose, but maybe it's better if you put a little distance between yourself and here for the next few days. Just please do me a favor and check in every now and then, would you, so I don't worry any more than I already am?"

If she didn't know Eli as she did, if she hadn't heard his side of things, hadn't felt his arms close around her, cherishing her, perhaps Chad's impassioned arguments would have persuaded her. Blinded her.

But she did know and had heard. Had felt her world shift and settle in Eli's embrace.

"I will." It was all she could manage through a throat gone thick with longing and fear, sorrow and desperate hope. "My father will still be dead, even if you put someone in jail. Maybe the risk isn't worth it." *Please, please, leave Eli alone.*

"Babe, you don't have to fret about me, but I love that you do."

Perhaps that illusion could serve a purpose, so she didn't argue. "Be careful, Chad."

"I will if you will. Bye, babe." He clicked off.

Don't call me babe. She barely resisted the urge to slam down the receiver.

"Lover boy staking his claim?"

She whirled at the sound of Eli's voice. "Oh—you scared me."

He crossed the room in two long strides, his chest and feet bare, clad only in jeans not fully buttoned. His blue eyes blazed. "What did he want?" No tender lover now, he gripped her shoulder with the hand of his good arm. "And why are you telling him to be careful?"

"You're hurting me." She shook him off. "What's wrong with you?"

"Wrong with me?" The blaze roared into an inferno. "You're all cozy with the man who would be happy to kill me. Whose father framed me and who's determined to do the same—"

She stepped around him.

He blocked her path.

"Eli—" She noticed, then, the heightened color. The glassy eyes. She felt his forehead. "You're burning up. Get back into bed."

"Not until you explain—" He faltered. "Oh, God. What am I doing? I'm sorry— you were just—"

She slipped under his good right arm. "Yeah. 'How good an actress are you?' Pretty good, I'd say, wouldn't you?"

"Gaby, I'm—"

"Sorry. I know." As her heart settled, she glanced up. Managed a grin.

"And jealous as hell. Even if he wasn't out to do away with me, I'd have to hate him simply because he'd give anything to be where I was last night, in your arms. Your bed." He gripped her waist and yanked her close. "I went a little crazy, thinking he might win."

"He wouldn't." She snuggled into him. "I wish you weren't feverish."

"It's you, not the wound."

She snickered. "Sure it is."

"I'm serious." He buried his face in her hair. "I burn for you, Gaby. Last night was…"

"Yeah." She didn't have the words, either, so for a moment, she simply relished the closeness.

"You're all my dreams rolled up into one, Gabriela Lucía Navarro," he whispered in her ear.

She melted.

"If only I could have you…" he murmured.

Suddenly, he sagged as if all the starch had gone out of him. She struggled to get him back to the bed. "Eli, come on. You have to help me. I'll get the pickup. I'm taking you to a doctor."

"No." He rallied. "I can't. Tomorrow night I have to—"

"You're not doing anything but lying in this bed and healing." She settled him on the mattress, her heart pounding with fear.

He grasped her hand. "No doctor. Just tired. Got to sleep. Give me more antibiotic."

"I'll give you a knot on the head, you stubborn jackass," she muttered, fighting her terror.

"That's my girl." He smiled, and his eyelids drifted shut.

Gaby raced for the pack with the syringe and precious vial. She filled it as he'd taught her, then struggled to budge over two hundred pounds of dead weight while she lowered his jeans. "I hope this hurts, you stupid, hardheaded—" She swiped at the tears leaking from her eyes and struggled to steady her shaking hand.

She held her breath as she pushed the needle in and depressed the plunger. Carefully, she rolled him to his back and tenderly covered him.

And watched him for a long time, each

and every rise and fall of that chest encasing the heart that kept her own beating.

ELI WAS STARVING. For the first time since he'd been shot, his head wasn't fuzzy. He started to rise, then registered the form beside him.

Gaby was fast asleep, her hand lightly touching his side, so small and slender, yet strong well beyond its size.

Just like her lion's heart.

He wanted to touch her, to draw her into him. To sink into the unbearable sweetness of her. To circle her with his arms and his strength and his determination, to protect her with every fiber of his body.

But the only way to safeguard her was, once again, to leave her. What he'd heard of her side of the phone conversation and Chad's cell phone call earlier convinced him that Chad wouldn't wish to harm her. Whatever his crimes, he had loved Gaby before Eli had ever met her. Both of them had one goal in common: to get Gaby out of harm's way.

As he studied her precious face, he saw the cost caring for him had extacted from her. She was thinner than when she'd arrived. Dark smudges lay beneath her eyes, and exhaustion lined her frame.

He couldn't lock her away in some safe spot, much as he'd like to.

So he had to lead the danger away from her. Tonight was the night, and he had preparations to make. He had to leave before the sky lightened any more, then he would spend the day in his cave, resting.

He would tell Gaby—no, he would beg her—to catch the first plane. Since he was fairly certain she wouldn't listen, he would add another suggestion that could keep her out of harm's way: he'd request that she go to Alpine and try to find the safe-deposit box to match that key. If she uncovered the evidence Frank had been compiling, all to the good, but Eli would be gathering his own tonight at the drop point. He would ask her to meet him tomorrow night at the cave. Together, they'd journey to Fort Davis, out of Chad's jurisdiction, to give over what they had to the proper authorities.

Because his plans had altered. When he'd answered Frank's summons, he'd wanted revenge as much as a chance to clear his name, but Gaby had thrown a wild card into the game.

He hadn't cared, for a long time, if he lived or died. That was the secret of his *Hot Spot Journal*—he'd gone into all those dangerous places because his safety hadn't mattered all that much.

But now it did. Maybe last night was all they'd ever share, but he wanted to return her to her life safe and sound.

First move was to walk away from her now.

And so he did, praying with every step that he hadn't just had his last sight of her.

CHAPTER SIXTEEN

Please don't try to find me—you won't be able to, and you'll only arouse Chad's suspicions if you're spotted as you search.

Go home, Gaby, to New York. I swear I'll come to you when this is over.

You're frowning, I'd bet money. Maybe muttering some more about jackasses. Okay, I had to try. I really do wish you would leave and stay out of this.

But I know that thick head of yours and that stubborn heart. If you won't comply, I need your help. I promise I'll meet you tomorrow night at the cave. Please find out if that key opens a safe-deposit box in Alpine, as you think it does. Be careful. Make sure you're not followed. If you see any sign of surveillance, forget the key. I'm going to have my own evidence by the time we meet, so don't take any foolish chances.

Just stay safe, Gaby. Please. You hold all there has ever been of my heart.
Eli

"Idiot. Stupid, mule-headed—" She sank to the kitchen chair. "Oh, Eli, what have you done?" She resisted the urge to put her head down and weep.

Instead, she shoved herself to her feet, folded his note and tucked it inside her bra, next to her skin.

He was right, blast him. She didn't dare risk leading anyone to him. That didn't change how she would read him the riot act when she found him. He was hurt. He had no business being out there in his condition.

She walked to the sink, looked out at the vast expanse, aware that he could be anywhere out there. Could be faint, could be bleeding, could be—

She snapped her gaze from the sight, landed on the single plate and fork he'd washed and attempted to draw comfort from knowing he'd eaten the food she'd prepared for him. But all she could think was—

Please.

Blindly, she made her way to her mother's altar. Blew the dust off the candle and lit it. Withdrew the rosary in shaking fingers and struggled to remember how to pray. She summoned every saint she could recall, begged the Virgin for help, pleaded with all of them to guard Eli, to keep him from opening his wound, to give him the strength and cunning to survive whatever his plan was—

Bring him back to me. I realize it's selfish. I know I've strayed. I've made so many, many mistakes, but please, please don't let him pay for them.

Even if I can't have him back...let him survive. Set him free from the past that has haunted him for so long. Grant him the happiness he deserves more than anyone I've ever known.

Clutching the rosary, she placed her forehead to the altar. *Mama...Papa...help him.*

Long moments later, she rose, slipped the rosary over her head and extinguished the candle.

Then she went to her room to prepare.

ELI BREATHED A SIGH of relief as he trained the binoculars on the house and saw a dressed-to-the-nines Gaby emerge, headed, he hoped, for Alpine and the bank. It was possible that she wouldn't be allowed access, but he'd have to hope that Frank had anticipated that someone else might have to get into the box. Regardless that Frank and Gaby had been estranged, she still seemed the most logical person for Frank to trust, since any need for the box but his would likely mean that Frank would be unable to do so himself. As the only blood relative, Gaby was the obvious choice.

As he watched her go, he was slammed right back into reality by her appearance. Understated elegance in her trim black sheath, her hair slicked into a French twist, she was every inch the successful career woman. Not a trace left of the innocent girl he'd once loved or the jeans-clad woman who'd battled both his injury and her own fears in order to save him.

He didn't know this Gaby, what she was like, what she wanted...who, if anyone, she could love.

But she'd clung to him in the night, fed

him water from her own lips. Had wept when they'd made love.

Had fought the devil himself, more than once, for Eli's worthless soul.

And just might do so again.

Regardless, his course was set. He'd bluffed her successfully, it seemed, so he would hole up in his cave today to gather strength for the night, now that she'd gone.

And when darkness fell, he'd finish this miserable chapter of his life.

SURELY THERE WAS A magazine article in this: "City Girl Goes Undercover." Maybe her old dreams of being a writer hadn't all vanished. Opening bullet point: "How to Spot a Tail, Based on All the Spy Movies You've Ever Watched."

Her only saving grace was that the Trans Pecos was hardly overcrowded. Between Chamizal and Alpine, nearly two hours away, she might pass ten, maybe twenty cars. Even a neophyte could surely notice if the same one appeared behind her.

Of course, it might only be someone else headed to Alpine, for groceries or a doctor's appointment or…whatever.

Could she count on a bad guy looking like a bad guy?

Get a grip, Gaby. She was mostly playing mind games with herself to distract her from how worried she was about Eli. How mad she was at him for leaving her behind, blast him. This was no time to be a hero.

Except he couldn't help it. Eli was hero material, down to the bone. For the first time since he'd explained the situation to her, she had the time and space to ponder what had truly happened all those years ago.

He'd given her up in order to save her. Just as he'd denied himself the chance to be her first lover because it was best for her.

In his opinion, anyway. *Damn you, Eli— when are you going to let me think for myself?*

Mentally, she apologized. He'd had a far more intimate acquaintance with the dark side of life than even she had understood, close as they'd been. He, like her father, had shielded her from the harsh realities.

Oh, Papa. Grief struck her afresh as she contemplated how she'd lashed out at him for locking her in her room. For keeping her from Eli. He'd been trying, in the only way he could, to protect her, and she'd hurled bitter words at him.

The road before her blurred as she realized how alone he must have felt.

I could have handled the truth, Papa. I would have helped, if only you'd told me.

But could she have, really? Wrapped in the cocoon of his devotion, had she been strong or merely headstrong?

Heaven save her from overprotective men.

I'm sorry, Papa. I hope you can hear me. Maybe someday I'll deserve your forgiveness, but I can't imagine how.

At last, Alpine appeared in the distance. Gaby thrust away the past that haunted her and prepared herself to search for evidence that would help create a future for Eli.

AN HOUR AND A WHOLE LOT of patience later, Gaby emerged from the bank with a brown envelope full of papers in her hand, her heart racing at what she'd scanned in the privacy area of the vault.

Bless you, Papa, both for compiling this and for having the foresight to leave a note with permission for me to access the box.

She couldn't wait to read the whole

thing, but she wouldn't do that now. Everything in her ached to pore over it this second, in the hope that there would be no reason for Eli to hazard whatever he was doing tonight.

Please don't try to find me. I promise I'll meet you tomorrow night at the cave.

The hours until then would be endless. She decided to get gas before she left town and stop to buy more extensive groceries as a leap of faith that she would have another opportunity to feed Eli.

He needed fattening up. He was too lean.

Oh, Lordy… Gaby burst into giggles. She was the furthest thing from the *he-needs-fattening-up* type.

Look what you've done to me, Eli. Next thing I'll be wearing a ruffled apron.

She was still grinning to herself when she pulled into the grocery-store parking lot. She stopped in a shady spot at the edge of the pavement, knowing that wouldn't do much to keep the pickup cool, but anything would help. She stashed the brown envelope behind the seat, then emerged and locked the cab.

A hand clapped over her face, a strong

arm gripped her from behind. She struggled against the hold and the sickly sweet fumes—

Until darkness claimed her.

CHAPTER SEVENTEEN

ELI HUNKERED DOWN in his observation point, attempting to stem the unease he'd felt ever since he'd detoured on his way here to check on Gaby's return.

And had found her still gone.

The reasons could be many. She might have taken his advice and gone back to New York. Or perhaps the lure of civilization—however far Alpine was from Manhattan's level—proved too much to resist. Maybe the bank was giving her trouble, and she'd had no choice but to stay late and drive home after dark.

There were a million possibilities, many of them harmless. But even without her knowing exactly what he intended, she was aware that he had plans tonight and that they entailed risk.

The woman who'd battled to keep him

alive would have come back at the first opportunity, even understanding that she couldn't locate him until he was ready to be found. She would still want to be close.

He heard engines in the distance and forced his mind to the present. There was nothing he could do for Gaby now. God willing, she would be there when he was done.

Man, he was ready for this to be over.

He'd spent much time as an observer, little as a warrior. There were any number of men he'd met hc could wish at his side, but that was not his fate now. He was on his own, as he had been much of his life.

To settle himself, he double-checked his weapons: the 9 mm at his hip, the .32 at his ankle, the Gerber knife at his waist. He'd already tested the night-vision camera.

Then he spotted the headlamps of the trucks, disguised as they were by louvered shields. A moonless night like this, though the traditional favorite of smugglers, was hell on night-vision lenses. Too little ambient light for them to gather optimal images, necessitating the use of an infrared flashlight to help identify faces or license plates. Identification and documentation were all he could expect to manage, only one man and in his less-than-optimal condition.

He hoped to hell it would be enough. He yearned to be free of all this, to clear his name, to have Frank's killer identified and arrested. It was too late to do the same for his mother.

For her, he would live, and that would be his vengeance. His tribute.

And if he was very lucky, he would have at least a little more time with Gaby.

The thought of her stirred his unease again. His plan would have him out of here in a couple of hours and back at the cave, but instead of waiting out the day to meet her the following night, he decided he would slip away in dawn's murky light and find her. Wake her with kisses. Steal her from this place and rendezvous with authorities who would handle it from there. Finish this, so he and Gaby could go on with their lives.

The trucks rumbled nearer, headed north toward the waiting cargo vans he'd already photographed. Their drivers had yet to emerge.

An unexpected engine could be heard

from the west. Eli slipped deeper into the vegetation and out of the path of this new set of headlights not so thoroughly disguised. He frowned, unsure what was happening, but at that moment, the first northbound truck rolled to a stop.

Eli lifted his camera and began filming again, wishing he could get closer to be certain that the audio was sufficient. He kept his own breaths as shallow as possible so that his respirations wouldn't mask the conversations much farther away.

The second truck hadn't yet arrived when the back of the first opened, disgorging its load.

Women. Girls, really, Asian girls so young some could not have entered puberty yet. He caught snippets of conversation in Cambodian, which he knew a little, and what he believed to be Chinese, though he spoke hardly any of that. Vietnamese, as well, a jumble of frightened voices from terrified, dirty faces, most of them cowed and confused, some bruised and all so emaciated that his gorge rose.

He'd witnessed much suffering in his travels. He understood how much of the world did not share American values and emphasis on the importance of the individual, but the human capacity for cruelty never ceased to astonish and sicken him.

Everything in him craved to race down this hillock and make the bastards pay. No one should be able to rationalize trafficking in human slavery.

He would only become one of the prisoners, however, and solve nothing, save no one. So he kept filming, documenting each face, hoping that his efforts would help free these women one day soon.

But while he filmed, he burned.

From the cargo vans, crates marked as weapons were unloaded, then shifted to the big trucks, while the human cargo was jammed into the vans, likely with no water and no food. These people would have been locked in containers on ships, then brought overland from the Mexican coast or up through Central America. They'd probably journeyed for weeks now on subsistence nutrition only, and some of them would have already died, though the traffickers would keep that number to a minimum. They were paid by the head, after all.

Like cattle, only livestock were shown more mercy. Eli steeled himself to continue, but in his agitation, he shifted slightly and, balance fouled by his bad arm, dislodged a small shower of rocks.

He froze. Only one man seemed to notice.

But that one man lifted a radio to his mouth, and Eli knew the jig was up. He had to decamp quickly or lose all he'd gathered this night.

"Wolverton—" an unfamiliar voice, heavily accented, shouted from below. "Show yourself."

Shocked to hear his name called, still he moved with all the stealth possible, seeking the best path.

"We have what you would call a trump card," said the man he still didn't recognize. "I suggest you have a look before you decide to vanish."

Dread balled in his gut. Eli rose barely enough to see and not enough to be spotted, but once he got a glimpse, nothing else mattered.

There, in the headlights of the recent arrival, gagged and bound—

Stood Gaby. Face bruised. Clothing torn.

DON'T DO IT, ELI, Gaby tried to scream against her gag. *If you're out there, run!* She struggled in her captor's hold.

He slapped her. "Shut up!"

She prayed that Eli hadn't witnessed the blow. She could only imagine his rage if he had. She wished she could fight the man herself, but he was twice her size and her thrashing about would only result in further provocation for Eli to reveal his position.

Eli was strong, but he was injured and severely outnumbered. Their only chance lay in his self-control.

"What kind of man lets his woman take his punishment?" her captor roared. "He is no man at all, do you not think so, Rico?"

One of the other men laughed. They swore and insulted Eli in Spanish, in which he was fluent. With every taunt, her spirits sank.

She looked around her at the vans being loaded up, some already zooming off, and wondered exactly what was being smuggled. Then, in the partially open rear of the last one, she saw.

Illegal immigrants, she thought at first, then realized they were not Hispanic. She got a closer view and spotted the bound hands, the rail-thin frames, the tilted eyes.

Oh, my God. All women and girls. She felt sick. The sex trade? Outrage swamped her. She jerked, but her captor's grip only tightened. "Be still—"

Desperate to escape, to help, she drew back her foot and kicked hard at the side of his knee as she'd been taught in self-defense class.

He went down with a roar, hauling her with him. He reared above her, arm cocked to slam his fist in her face.

Behind his back, she spotted a figure vaulting over the top of the rise, still in shadow. Her heart sank. *No, Eli, no—*

A pickup screeched to a stop beside them. The driver's door opened, and a man charged, weapon drawn. "What the hell are you doing, Pablo? Get off her—now!"

Chad. For once, she was thrilled to see him.

Her captor's head whipped around at Chad's cry. The man who must be Pablo leaped to his feet with surprising quickness and yanked her to standing in front of him, brandishing his own weapon. "I'm cleaning up your mess, Anderson. She found the papers her father had hidden. You were too busy panting after her to do your job, so I will."

Oh, no. Eli was right. Chad is part of this. The knowledge sickened her.

"Let her go." Chad's face was filled with fury as he scanned her face. "Or I'll blow your head off."

Her captor simply turned the muzzle and jammed it into her temple. "I don't think so. Drop your weapon."

"No way. Carlos—" Chad yelled. "Get the trucks moving. You stay behind."

"*Sí, jefe.*" The man stepped from behind the lead van. He issued rapid orders, and the vans and trucks quickly dispersed.

"You're outnumbered, Pablo," Chad said. "Let her go."

"You should learn to count better, Sheriff," Pablo said, sneering.

Gaby glanced over and noticed that the man named Carlos had his weapon trained not on her captor but on Chad.

Chad's eyes widened when he spotted the same thing. "Carlos, our fathers worked together. We're friends." He shot a glance at Gaby, but she couldn't read his expression.

Nonetheless, she readied herself. Maybe she could unbalance her captor again and give Chad an edge.

"Your lust for this woman has blinded you, *compadre.*" The muzzle jammed harder into her temple.

Then Carlos spoke up. "Your father was a bastard, Chad. He stole from his crew. He killed my uncle, one of his own men. I owe you nothing."

"Do not move again, *amigo,*" Pablo said.

She observed Chad edging away, perhaps to get a better shot. Despite everything he might have done, she couldn't stand for him to be killed.

Eli, where are you?

"Hey! You— Pablo—" Eli called out.

Her captor whirled, and the gun at her temple wavered. She heard a faint report, and the man beside her jolted as if struck, began to fall, dragging her with him—

She battled to keep her feet, but his weight was too much for her. She landed with a thud. Her captor collapsed on top of her.

More shots, a hail of them.

She tried to scramble away from her captor, but he was deadweight, pinning her.

"Gaby, stay down—" Eli yelled.

A shout of pain beside her. A falling body. Everywhere, gunfire. She couldn't see— Couldn't breathe—

Eli, she screamed against her gag. *Oh, please not Eli—*

She shoved and pushed, desperate to wriggle free, to find out if the man she loved was alive or dead.

The unbearable weight was suddenly lifted. Someone grabbed her arm. She fought him—

"Shh-shh, Gaby. Hush, it's me."

"Eli?"

He stripped away her gag, then went to work on her hands.

"Yes, sweetheart, it's me." His voice was unsteady. "How bad are you hurt?"

"I'm okay—"

Then her hands were free, and he yanked her into his embrace.

"Are you hit, Eli?" She raced her shaking hands over him.

"No."

"Oh, thank God." She reached for his face. Flung her arms around him and held on for dear life.

Eli's embrace tightened, too. "Okay," he said. "We're okay. But we have to move, Gaby."

Then she realized that everything was silent. "Are they gone? Is everyone—" She couldn't seem to quit shivering.

Then behind her, she heard a moan and turned. Gasped.

"Chad. Eli, it's Chad." She scrambled over to him.

Chad lay on the ground a few feet away, his face a mask of agony. In the headlights from his truck, she spotted dark wet, dark pools all around him.

"Oh, no— Eli, we have to help him."

Eli bent over Chad, his face grim.

"Gabriela." Chad's voice was barely audible. "I never meant—"

"Chad, don't talk. We'll get you to a doctor."

"Too…late." His breaths were shallow pants. "Leave…now. They'll come…back." He looked past her at Eli. "Get her…out."

Whatever he'd done wrong, she couldn't simply walk away. They'd meant something to each other once.

"Chad—" She clasped his hand between hers. "You can make it. Don't give up—"

"No time—" he gasped. "Eli. Dad...lied."

"Of course he did." she spoke before Eli could. "Eli was innocent. But why, Chad? How did you get involved with this?"

A faint smile crossed his lips. "Show Dad...who was...better son."

"What?" She frowned. "What do you mean?"

He didn't answer, staring beyond her at Eli, who stood frozen. A shiver ran through her.

Eli shook his head violently. Reeled back in horror. "No. God, no."

Chad's nod was barely visible. "Yes. Half... brothers. Put you...in his will. Didn't...want to share."

"What?" Even in the poor light, she could see Eli's face drained of all color. "No. He hated me. He wouldn't—"

Chad tried to laugh, but instead, a horrible gurgle emerged. "But respected... your guts. Beat me...too. Said I...spoiled... weak—" He choked, and blood spilled from between his lips.

"Chad!" she cried. Faced Eli. "What can we do? Where's your pack?"

But Eli was focused on Chad, his face filled with both confusion and sorrow.

She twisted, bent over the man on the ground. Watched him go still, his eyes grow sightless. "No! Chad, no—"

Eli stirred. Knelt and felt for a pulse. "He's gone." His voice was a monotone.

"But—" She wrestled to make sense of what had happened.

Eli stirred. "We have to leave. The sound of gunshots travels. As he said, someone will come back."

She stared down at the man who'd once been a golden boy, the adored child who'd had everything. Thought about the shocking revelations. "Your... brother? I can't—"

Eli's face had gone stone still again. "That sick bastard." His eyes were pure devastation.

The radio in Chad's truck crackled and forced them back to the moment. The danger that wasn't over.

She examined Chad's unmoving form. "What do we do about—"

"Nothing."

"He tried to help me. He cared about me once," she whispered. "He's your family."

The sound of an engine broke the night.

"You're my only concern now." Eli

grabbed her arm. "We'll notify the authorities about where he is, once I have you safely away." He moved quickly beyond the circle of light. She had no choice but to follow.

They traveled swiftly, Eli as though to outrun the terrible revelations. Gaby's shoes were unsuited to the terrain, but she remained silent and did her best to keep up with him, wondering how to help him deal with what must be shattering news. She was reeling herself, struggling to put the pieces together in light of what Chad had said.

She assumed they were headed to the cave, but in the moonless dark, she had to depend on Eli's guidance as he used his night-vision goggles to navigate. After what felt like hours, she was shocked to find her house in sight.

At the back door, he halted. "Where are the papers?"

"Behind the seat in Papa's pickup at the grocery store in Alpine."

His jaw flexed. "They hurt you."

"I'm fine. Just a few blisters and some sore muscles."

He saw her shoes and swore. "Why didn't you say something?"

"What were you going to do, carry me when you're injured much worse? Come inside, Eli. Let me check your dressings."

He shook his head. "I have to go."

"Where?"

"To—" He glanced to the side. "I don't know. I've got to think." He looked at her. "Lock up. Don't open for anyone until you hear from me. If someone calls you with the news about Chad, pretend it's a surprise. I'll get the pickup back to you as soon as I can." He turned away.

"Are you crazy?" She grasped his good arm. "Wherever you go, I'm right behind you." She gentled her voice as the anguish on his face registered. "Eli, you need food and sleep. We have to talk about this."

"I can't—" He stood stiff as a statue. "I don't—"

"I love you."

His head jerked up. In his eyes was both yearning and rage. "When I might have that murdering bastard's blood in my veins? When you understand what evil I come from? That I have absolutely nothing to offer you?" His voice rose to a roar. "How can you possibly love me when I'm—when I'm—"

He was strung so tight he was shaking.

Gaby wrapped her arms around him and held on. "Blood doesn't matter. I know who you are, Eli Wolverton. I've seen into your soul. You're a valiant man who has triumphed over—"

"You know nothing—" He whirled to pace, raking his fingers through his hair. "Go back to New York. You have a life there. A future. Dreams you've wanted since you were a kid. With me, you'll have none of them."

His insistence was knotting her stomach. "I was a girl when I had those notions. Then I was a lonely woman who had nothing else. Is there no compromise in you, Eli? Do you want to be forever the lone wolf standing outside the glow of the campfire?"

His silence filled her with dread. "I'm tainted, Gaby. I hope to God Chad was wrong, because I don't think I can bear it if that man is my father. I used to long to have a family, but—" His voice went hoarse as he gazed at her with yearning. "How can I smear an innocent child with the blood of a man who beat me, who murdered my mother, who trafficked in human suffering?"

"You aren't him. What he was has nothing to do with you." She approached him again, and when he backed away, she crowded him. "You are a good person, despite all the odds that were stacked against you. Chad had everything given to him and didn't do half as much with his life as you've managed when granted not even the minimum of resources or hope or love. When you were abused and abandoned as no child should be."

She raised her hand to his cheek, desperate for contact. "I have only one dream that matters, Eli."

"What is it?" His voice was rusty with longing.

"Your love. For the rest of my life."

"I will love you until the day I die." He was so terribly solemn. "But that changes nothing."

Though her heart was aching, she persisted. "You're wrong."

"We're different. Too different. I don't like cities, and you love them. You're gold and I'm...dirt. You have ambition and possibilities. I have..." He spread his hands, helpless. "Not one thing to bring to you."

"There's your heart."

He shook his head. "Not good enough."

She had the sense that if she pushed him now, he would vanish and she would never find him again. She witnessed the war within him and understood that all her words might not be sufficient to overcome what haunted him. That she could still lose him and spend the rest of her life without the love that was her heart's reason for being. Without the other half of her soul.

Balanced on the razor's edge, she realized just how exhausted she was.

How much more drained he must be.

Though she was terrified of a misstep, she took a chance and backed off. "At least let me check your injuries."

"I need to get the rest of this settled first. I'm a fugitive, and I have to turn myself in."

"But—"

"Yes," he said firmly. "It all begins with that. I want a clean slate. A new chapter."

"I'll go with you."

"No."

"Don't disappear again, Eli," she pleaded, caring little for dignity now. "Come back to me when you're done, and let's talk. Please."

"There's no point."

"You could give this up, what's between us? Just…walk away once more?"

Torment flickered. "Gaby, you're refusing to accept the truth."

"What truth?" Heartache flipped to fury. "That you're running away again?"

"As you've done for all these years?" he thundered. "There are people right here in Chamizal who need that brain of yours, that heart and courage. I've seen more suffering than you can imagine, and I know I can't stop all of it, but at least I'm doing something, bringing attention to their plights. You're doing articles on how to use Botox and get highlighted when there are women being sold into slavery or beaten by bastards like—"

He halted, breathing hard. "I'm sorry. Forget it. You're not to blame, I'm just—" He stared into the distance.

Stricken, she couldn't summon a response. What he'd said put her own recent doubts into focus. Shed light on the unease that had gnawed at her for some time.

He stirred. "You didn't deserve that. You haven't been where I've gone, haven't seen—"

"But you're right. I have some decisions to make, about this place, my career…" She bit her lip to keep from saying *you*. She straightened her shoulders. "I'll be here for three more days. Eli, please—" She held his gaze, hoping to glimpse even a trace of what they'd shared. "What we have is something most people only dream of. Maybe you're correct that it's not enough. But you're not a coward, so I dare you to grant us a chance."

His expression was both fond and desperately sad. "You could do much better than me, Gaby. The world is full of men who would fight like hell to have a woman like you."

"What about you?" Defeat crept over her, but she couldn't seem to stop. "Will you relinquish me so easily?"

"There's nothing easy about it, honey." He reached out for her, but retracted his hand before he could touch. "I have to leave," he said softly. "Goodbye, Gaby."

And he began walking in the direction of his cave.

"I'll wait for you, Eli," she called after him.

But if he heard, he gave no sign of it. She

watched him until his form vanished into the darkness.

Stood there until the chill air invaded her bones.

A sound at her feet roused her. "Hey, Buddy." She dropped to her knees and buried her face in his fur. "He left you, too, huh?"

It was then that she was certain he would not be back.

REGARDLESS, SHE LINGERED an extra day, but he didn't show. She was busy during that interval, cleaning and packing the house. She decided to allow herself some time to figure out what to do with the ranch and made arrangements for Ramón's grandson to move some livestock onto the land in exchange for caring for the property. With her new raise, she could afford to pay the taxes on the place for a while and not dip into her father's modest savings if she didn't get that new, bigger apartment.

She debated about bringing Buddy with her, craving to hold on to that one last link to Eli, but in the end, she left him with Ramón. Cooping him up in the city wasn't fair to the dog, anymore than it would have been to Eli. In that, Eli was right about the differences between her and him.

But she wasn't ready to give up on Eli. Or to sever her last tie with the place of her birth. She left her address and phone numbers with Juanita, just in case he changed his mind. The old woman's sympathy had both wounded and touched her.

"I don't know what he will do, child. This new information has hit him hard, and he's struggling."

Gaby managed to resist, only barely, asking Juanita to tell her where he was.

But the next move was up to him. And she had her own thinking to do.

So it was that, with fall crisp in the air, she arrived back in New York just over a week after she'd left, though the interim felt like a lifetime. She heard the constant din that had once been so exciting and couldn't help contrasting it with the deep silence of a West Texas night. She looked around the tiny apartment and felt the walls pressing in, the impulse to turn around and run back out.

But she had nowhere else to go.

The phone rang, and for an instant her heart lifted. Maybe it was—

She picked up the receiver, breathless with hope. "Hello?"

"Hey, girl, welcome home!" Beth said. "How are you, my friend?"

Tears nearly blinded her. "I'm—" *Okay,* she meant to say. But she couldn't.

And Beth seemed to hear. "I'm on my way."

"Thank you." Gaby dropped her head into her hands as despair swamped her, fought the urge to curl up in a corner.

Then she forced herself to remove her coat, hang it up and begin unpacking.

Time to go on with the life she'd put so much effort into creating.

AN ENDLESS, DREARY WEEK of sleepless nights later, she sat in her first editorial board meeting, where she'd dreamed of being for so long. Across the table, discussion raged over whether to feature a Botox article or one on a newer type of nonsurgical face-lift.

And all Gaby could hear was Eli's challenge in her head. "What about an article on the sex trade?"

Heads swiveled toward her, eyebrows raised high. A ponderous silence descended, but she forged onward. "There are women being brought into this country as sex slaves. Isn't that more important than plastic surgery?"

Beth's expression was filled with sympathy. The others ranged from polite cynicism to outright astonishment. The features editor peered down her nose at Gaby as though she'd smelled something bad.

Someone behind Gaby snickered.

"Botox has been done to death," the features editor continued as if Gaby had never spoken. "Let's go with this new laser technique."

Every gaze shifted from Gaby. Instant pariah. Beth bit her lip and conveyed an unspoken message of support, but Gaby was clear that she'd made a serious faux pas. She was a member of this group in name only; she hadn't earned her stripes yet. She could be replaced in a heartbeat with any number of bright young things teeming on the small island of Manhattan. No one would remember her for long.

She could, of course, recover from this gaffe by working very hard. She might still one day replace her boss as she'd meant to.

But, she wondered, how much of herself would she give up to do so?

There are people right here in Chamizal who need that brain of yours, that heart and courage.

Something within her stirred. Stretched. Scented the tang of creosote bushes, recalled the wind blowing over her skin, the sun painting her face. Drawing in a breath, so clean, so deep in her blood—-

It was then that she understood what she must do.

She had fled Chamizal and its people because she'd believed she was missing out, that around the next corner there would be excitement and glitter and accolades. Treasures to be unearthed. She'd considered Chamizal and her life there a trap, her past a prison.

But she'd been free for years, and what had it gained her? Loneliness, isolation in the middle of millions, absurd attempts to remake herself in someone else's image? To leave behind her heritage and all that had made her strong enough to tackle Manhattan.

Back in West Texas were her people. Her roots. Yes, she was intelligent and capable and ambitious, but why must those attributes be used only in a city? Why should they serve only her?

You could flee or you could stand your ground. You could fight your way to the top, or you could battle to help others make it. What she'd learned in the nine years after she'd left Chamizal—about life, about the system and how to work it, about failure and success and believing in yourself—these things she could pass along to children such as Linda's...or even her own. However unreal the prospect of having children with anyone but Eli felt.

"Gaby?" Her boss's sharp voice intruded. "What?"

"I asked you a question about the April issue."

Automatically, Gaby began to shuffle through her files to retrieve her notes—

Then she halted. What was the point?

But inside, she shivered. Could she really walk away from this? Was she insane? The moment strung out on a filament so fine, a wayward breath could snap it.

"Gaby? Are you prepared?"

The question was more far-reaching than her boss could have imagined.

You're not a coward, she'd told Eli. But what of herself?

Slowly, she stood. Exchanged one glance with a bewildered Beth, then proceeded to outline what would have seemed a brilliant layout only weeks before.

The board, for the most part, appeared impressed with her ideas, though some refinements were suggested. As she listened and discussed, a part of her stood separate, observing the scene with more than a little regret over what she was about to do. What would never be.

But already, remorse was being replaced by a lighter heart. The inner click that told you you were on the right path.

When the meeting adjourned, before she could lose her nerve, she asked her boss for a minute alone.

"I want to thank you for giving me a chance. This has been an exciting time in my life, and I'm so grateful for your encouragement." She paused. Sucked in her breath. "But I've decided to return to West

Texas. I don't expect you to understand my choice."

"You're right about that. How can you leave all this? What will you do?"

She laughed. "Not exactly sure. I have a degree in communications with a minor in business. There are people out there who should have their voices heard on a variety of topics, but in truth…I'm going to have to wing it." Thank goodness she would at least have a roof over her head and a little money her father had tucked away.

"You're bright and energetic, Gaby, and you're ambitious. You'll miss this."

"Likely, I will. But New York's not going anywhere, and planes fly both ways. I know young girls who need a sense of the wider world, and boys who deserve to have someone show them the ropes. To give them confidence that they're as good as anyone educated in an Ivy League school."

She spread her hands and shook her head. "I'm sure it sounds like I'm off my rocker, but when I left Chamizal, I realized that I can be useful there in a way I never could here. I wish you all well, and I will never forget any of this, but—" Her heart was racing, and she was caught between delight and disbelief that she was actually doing this.

"It's time for me to go home."

AS GABY WALKED BACK TO her office, musing over the expression on her boss's face, she laid a hand over her jittery stomach. As excited as she was, she was also terrified of the risk she was taking.

"What was that about?" Beth spoke from behind her. "You okay?"

"I am." Gaby smiled. "I quit."

Beth's eyes popped. "You…what? Have you lost your mind?"

"Maybe. Probably." Giddy and breathless, she grasped her friend's shoulders and waltzed Beth into her office, talking too fast to outrun her terror. "I don't know how to explain to you, but it feels right." Then reality hit her. "Oh, Beth, I will miss you so much. I'll never see you again, will I?"

They'd been each other's lifelines in a pressure-packed situation. Gaby wasn't sure how she'd manage without her friend, or vice versa.

Then Beth shook her head and exhaled hard. "Scorpions, right? Tarantulas, snakes?"

"But there's also—"

A peal of laughter issued. "Never mind the sales job. Of course I'll visit." She paused. "At least once." She winked. "Toss in a hot cowboy or two, and I could be a regular." She threw her arms around Gaby and hugged her hard.

Gaby heard her sniffing and was close to tears herself. "I could tell when you got back," Beth murmured. "So are you going after the loner?"

Eli. Gaby was too raw to think about him, yet all of a sudden, he filled her mind. "No," she said. "It's up to him now. He has to take that first step."

"If not, he doesn't deserve you." Beth hugged her fiercely, then stepped away. "Okay, how long do I have to plan the going-away bash of the century?"

"Two weeks." At the words, her stomach did a flip. "Oh, Lordy."

But Beth was already halfway out the door, muttering party details to herself.

For the next few hours, Gaby made lists and phone calls to cover the million details of relocation. She had her hair grasped in one hand while she scribbled yet another to-do item.

"Gaby?" The receptionist. "You have a visitor."

Gaby held up one hand and kept writing. "I don't have any appointments."

"I didn't call ahead." The voice was deep and as familiar to Gaby as her own.

She glanced up. The pen dropped from her fingers. "Eli—" She fell speechless. Was she hallucinating?

They stared at each other.

"God, you're beautiful." He leaned against the door frame, no apparent discomfort from his injured shoulder.

She barely noticed the receptionist leaving. "Your arm is better?"

"Yeah. I had a good surgeon."

"Don't give me nightmares." She shuddered. "I never want to do anything remotely like that again."

"But you could, that's the thing. You'll manage whatever's thrown at you."

He'd always had faith in her, a gift beyond price.

But the questions tumbled in her head: *Do I have to manage without you? Do you feel any of what I do?*

What on earth are you doing here?

Another silence, more awkward than the first.

Finally, he spoke. "Don't you want to ask me where the devil I've been?"

"I...yes. I do."

"I spent quite a while with the Texas Ranger who's in charge of the case. Discovered I'd never been formally charged and that I was free to go, as long as they could get in touch with me."

"I'm so glad, Eli." And she was.

"He may have to talk to you, but for now, your father's papers are enough, he said."

She shrugged. "I'll be around."

He went quiet again.

"Then—" A line appeared between his brows. "I gathered up my gear and made it all the way to LAX, ready to buy a ticket to Nepal." He cast a sideways glance at her. "Lots going on there these days."

"Really."

"Yeah." He straightened. Stepped away from the door.

Closer to her. "But instead, I found myself booking a flight to La Guardia."

She felt a little breathless. "Why?"

He shifted uneasily. "Gaby, I don't know

the steps of this dance. I—" He looked around, anywhere but at her. "You're settled in here. I still don't have much to offer you, not compared with all this."

That startled a small laugh from her. "You might be surprised." She picked up a stack of papers from her desk, held them out.

He frowned. "What's that?"

"Lists of what to pack."

His eyes widened. "Why?"

"I'm—" She spread her hands. "Going home. As you pointed out, it's my heritage. My roots."

"For real?" He shook his head. Then chuckled. "Unbelievable."

"What's so funny?" She took offense.

He saw it. "Because—" He shook his head. "I traveled here on a long shot. To see if I could convince you to return to Chamizal with me."

"You're kidding." She blinked. "Eli, why would you ever go there, of all places? After all that's happened?"

"I can't tell you I have it all worked out, but—" He spread his palms. "The Anderson ranch is mine, if I accept it. At first I couldn't. It's built on blood money, and I didn't want anything to do with that bastard.

"But then I had this idea." He moved in on her, and she could hear excitement shift into his voice. "I've traveled thousands of miles trying to raise awareness of suffering by documenting it, but that's too indirect." He ran his hands down her arms and gripped her fingers. "I don't have it all figured out, but there's plenty of hardship right where we grew up, and now I have acres and acres of space at my disposal.

"I've thought a lot about my mother and how she was trapped by circumstance. By him." His eyes went cold. "She needed options no one could give her. So it occurred to me that I had room to create a place for abused women and children to seek refuge. To learn useful skills as part of a working ranch." He smiled ruefully. "Of course, I'd have a lot of skills to master, too, but the ranch is solid. And what better way to avenge my mother and everyone else Bill Anderson harmed, than by using his empire to make others like them stronger?"

"That's—" She shook her head in admiration. "Amazing."

"Yeah? Not just crazy?"

"It's wonderful, Eli. Truly."

"So—" His gaze darted away. "Any chance you'd want to go in on it with me?"

"Me? You're after a business partner?"

"No. I mean, of course you'd be one hell of an example for those women to follow, and no one's smarter than you. But I'm holding out for more."

He drew her hands to his chest, and his grip betrayed nerves. "There's this woman who told me that I was a good person. That she had one dream that mattered more than anything else. I said she was nuts, and she is, but—"

He stopped. Swallowed hard. "Now that I've got that clean slate, I thought I might see if she would want to write a new story on it. With me."

She couldn't move, struggling to absorb that the barriers that had separated them for so many years were gone.

"I'm pretty sure she would." Her voice broke.

He gathered her into his arms. Held on tight. "I'm gonna make sure that this time, there's a happy ending," he murmured into her ear. "That I never have to leave you again."

"Oh, Eli—" She raised a tear-blurred gaze to his. Laid her hand on his cheek. "I do love you."

He took her hand, placed a kiss to her palm. "You have always been the one shining star in a dark life. I'll devote the rest of my days to making you happy. Will you marry me, Gabriela Lucía? Make a home with me, have a family? Even if it's nine years too late?"

Oh, Papa...this isn't exactly how you'd planned to unite these ranches and certainly not the Anderson son you had in mind, but—

Somehow, she thought he would approve.

"I waited for you, Eli." She slid her arms around him, determined to never let go. "Just as I promised."

"Thank God." He bent his head and kissed her deeply.

Gaby sank into his embrace, grateful, so grateful that at last, nothing would part her and this man who'd had too little love in his life. She would make his future so very different.

Suddenly, he lifted her high and twirled

her around. She tossed her head back and laughed for pure joy.

And in the hallway outside her door, applause and a sniff or two could be heard.

* * * * *

Dante Raintree stood with his arms crossed as he watched the woman on the monitor. The image was in black and white to better show details; color distracted the brain. He focused on her hands, watching every move she made, but what struck him most was how uncommonly still she was. She didn't fidget or play with her chips, or look around at the other players. She peeked once at her down card, then didn't touch it again, signaling for another hit by tapping a fingernail on the table. Just because she didn't seem to be paying attention to the other players, though, didn't mean she was as unaware as she seemed.

"What's her name?" Dante asked.

"Lorna Clay," replied his chief of security, Al Rayburn.

"At first I thought she was counting, but she doesn't pay enough attention."

"She's paying attention, all right," Dante murmured. "You just don't see her doing it." A card counter had to remember every card played. Supposedly counting cards was impossible with the number of decks used by the casinos, but there were those rare individuals who could calculate the odds even with multiple decks.

"I thought that, too," said Al. "But look at this piece of tape coming up. Someone she knows comes up to her and speaks, she looks around and starts chatting, completely misses the play of the people to her left—and doesn't look around even when the deal comes back to her, just taps that finger. And damn if she didn't win. Again."

Dante watched the tape, rewound it, watched it again. Then he watched it a third time. There had to be something he was missing, because he couldn't pick out a single giveaway.

"If she's cheating," Al said with something like respect, "she's the best I've ever seen."

"What does your gut say?"

Al scratched the side of his jaw, considering. Finally, he said, "If she isn't cheating, she's the luckiest person walking. She wins. Week in, week out, she wins. Never a huge amount, but I ran the numbers and she's into us for about five grand a week. Hell, boss, on her way out of the casino she'll stop by a slot machine, feed a dollar in and walk away with at least fifty. It's never the same machine, either. I've had her watched, I've had her followed, I've even looked for the same faces in the casino every time she's in here, and I can't find a common denominator."

"Is she here now?"

"She came in about half an hour ago. She's playing blackjack, as usual."

"Bring her to my office," Dante said, making a swift decision. "Don't make a scene."

"Got it," said Al, turning on his heel and leaving the security center.

Dante left, too, going up to his office. His face was calm. Normally he would leave it to Al to deal with a cheater, but he was curious. How was she doing it? There were a lot of bad cheaters, a few good ones, and every so often one would come along who was the stuff of which legends were made: the cheater who didn't get caught, even when people were alert and the camera was on him—or, in this case, her.

It was possible to simply be lucky, as most people understood luck. Chance could turn a habitual loser into a big-time winner. Casinos, in fact, thrived on that hope. But luck itself wasn't habitual, and he knew that what passed for luck was often something else: cheating. And there was the other kind of luck, the kind he himself possessed, but it depended not on chance but on who and what he was. He knew it was an innate power and not Dame Fortune's erratic smile. Since power like his was rare, the odds made it likely the woman he'd been watching was merely a very clever cheat.

Her skill could provide her with a very good living, he thought, doing some swift calculations in his head. Five grand a week equaled $260,000 a year, and that was just from his casino. She probably hit them all, careful to keep the numbers relatively low so she stayed under the radar.

He wondered how long she'd been taking him, how long she'd been winning a little here, a little there, before Al noticed.

The curtains were open on the wall-to-wall

window in his office, giving the impression, when one first opened the door, of stepping out onto a covered balcony. The glazed window faced west, so he could catch the sunsets. The sun was low now, the sky painted in purple and gold. At his home in the mountains, most of the windows faced east, affording him views of the sunrise. Something in him needed both the greeting and the goodbye of the sun. He'd always been drawn to sunlight, maybe because fire was his element to call, to control.

He checked his internal time: four minutes until sundown. Without checking the sunrise tables every day, he knew exactly when the sun would slide behind the mountains. He didn't own an alarm clock. He didn't need one. He was so acutely attuned to the sun's position that he had only to check within himself to know the time. As for waking at a particular time, he was one of those people who could tell himself to wake at a certain time, and he did. That talent had nothing to do with being Raintree, so he didn't have to hide it; a lot of perfectly ordinary people had the same ability.

He had other talents and abilities,

however, that did require careful shielding. The long days of summer instilled in him an almost sexual high, when he could feel contained power buzzing just beneath his skin. He had to be doubly careful not to cause candles to leap into flame just by his presence, or to start wildfires with a glance in the dry-as-tinder brush. He loved Reno; he didn't want to burn it down. He just felt so damn *alive* with all the sunshine pouring down that he wanted to let the energy pour through him instead of holding it inside.

This must be how his brother Gideon felt while pulling lightning, all that hot power searing through his muscles, his veins. They had this in common, the connection with raw power. All the members of the far-flung Raintree clan had some power, some heightened ability, but only members of the royal family could channel and control the earth's natural energies.

Dante wasn't just of the royal family, he was the Dranir, the leader of the entire clan. "Dranir" was synonymous with king, but the position he held wasn't ceremonial, it was one of sheer power. He was the oldest son of the previous Dranir, but he would have been passed over for the position if he hadn't also inherited the power to hold it.

Behind him came Al's distinctive knock on the door. The outer office was empty, Dante's secretary having gone home hours before. "Come in," he called, not turning from his view of the sunset.

The door opened, and Al said, "Mr. Raintree, this is Lorna Clay."

Dante turned and looked at the woman, all his senses on alert. The first thing he noticed was the vibrant color of her hair, a rich, dark red that encompassed a multitude of shades from copper to burgundy. The warm amber light danced along the iridescent strands, and he felt a hard tug of sheer lust in his gut. Looking at her hair was almost like looking at fire, and he had the same reaction.

The second thing he noticed was that she was spitting mad.

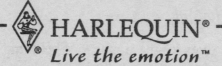

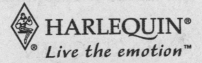

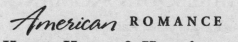
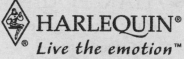

HARLEQUIN®
Presents®

**The world's bestselling romance series...
The series that brings you your favorite authors,
month after month:**

Helen Bianchin...Emma Darcy
Lynne Graham...Penny Jordan
Miranda Lee...Sandra Marton
Anne Mather...Carole Mortimer
Susan Napier...Michelle Reid

and many more uniquely talented authors!

Wealthy, powerful, gorgeous men...
Women who have feelings just like your own...
The stories you love, set in exotic, glamorous locations...

HARLEQUIN®
Presents®

Seduction and Passion Guaranteed!

HH Harlequin® Historical
Historical Romantic Adventure!

Imagine a time of chivalrous knights and unconventional ladies, roguish rakes and impetuous heiresses, rugged cowboys and spirited frontierswomen—— these rich and vivid tales will capture your imagination!

Harlequin Historical . . . they're too good to miss!